P.

Phoebe's eyes widened in shock; she still couldn't see Leo's face, but she could feel the pain emanating from him in sorrowful waves. 'Leo, I'm sorry.'

He turned his head, met her gaze. 'I couldn't let the same happen to you,' he continued, and Phoebe saw the honesty in his eyes. 'Even though I was tempted.'

'Tempted…?'

'You were an inconvenience, remember?' Leo gave her the ghost of a smile. 'At least I thought of you as one until I saw you again.'

Her heart bumped painfully against her ribs. She wanted to ask Leo what he meant, wanted to hope— *needed* to. But the future—her son's future—was too overwhelming.

'So what can we do?' she whispered. 'We can't—I can't—' She took a breath and started again, in a stronger voice. 'I won't be bought, and I won't leave my son.'

'I know.' Leo smiled, his mouth curling upwards in a way that made Phoebe's insides tingle with awareness. 'I have another solution.'

He paused, and in that second's silence Phoebe felt as if the room became hushed in expectation—as if everything had led to this moment, this question, this possibility. As if she already *knew*.

Leo took a step towards her, his hand outstretched. 'Phoebe,' he said, 'you can become my wife.'

Kate Hewitt discovered her first Mills & Boon® romance on a trip to England when she was thirteen, and she's continued to read them ever since. She wrote her first story at the age of five, simply because her older brother had written one and she thought she could do it too. That story was one sentence long—fortunately they've become a bit more detailed as she's grown older. She has written plays, short stories, and magazine serials for many years, but writing romance remains her first love. Besides writing, she enjoys reading, travelling, and learning to knit.

After marrying the man of her dreams—her older brother's childhood friend—she lived in England for six years and now resides in New York State, with her husband, her four young children, and the possibility of one day getting a dog. Kate loves to hear from readers—you can contact her through her website, www.kate-hewitt.com

ROYAL LOVE-CHILD, FORBIDDEN MARRIAGE

BY
KATE HEWITT

First published in Great Britain 2009
Harlequin Mills & Boon Limited,
Eton House, 18-24 Paradise Road, Richmond, Surrey TW9 1SR

© Kate Hewitt 2009

ISBN: 978 0 263 20842 9

Set in Times Roman 10½ on 12 pt
07-0909-48989

Harlequin Mills & Boon policy is to use papers that are natural, renewable and recyclable products and made from wood grown in sustainable forests. The logging and manufacturing process conform to the legal environmental regulations of the country of origin.

Printed and bound in Great Britain
by CPI Antony Rowe, Chippenham, Wiltshire

ROYAL LOVE-CHILD, FORBIDDEN MARRIAGE

To Aidan,
Thanks for being such a great friend—and fan!
Love, K

CHAPTER ONE

'How much?'

Phoebe Wells stared blankly at the man slouched in a chair across from her. He gazed back with a sensual smile and heavy-lidded eyes, his sable hair rumpled, the top two buttons of his shirt undone to reveal a smooth expanse of golden skin.

'How *much*?' she repeated. The question made no sense. How much what? Her fingers tightened reflexively around the strap of her bag and she tried not to fidget. She'd been hustled here by two government agents, and it had taken all her self-control not to ask if she was being arrested. Actually, it had taken all her self-control not to *scream*.

They'd given her no answers, not even a look, as they ushered her into one of the palace's empty reception rooms to wait for twenty panic-laden minutes before this man— Leo Christensen, Anders's cousin—had made his lazy entrance. And now he was asking her how much, and she had no idea what any of it meant.

She wished Anders were here; she wished he hadn't left her to suffer the scorn of his damnable cousin, the man who now uncoiled himself from the chair and rose to stand in front of her with an easy, lethal grace. She wished, she realised with a little pulse of panic, that she knew him better.

'How much money, Little Miss Golddigger?' Leo Christensen clarified softly. 'Just how much money will it take to make you leave my cousin alone?'

Shock stabbed her with icy needles, but it was soon replaced by an even icier calm. Of course. She should have expected this; she knew the Christensen family—the royal family of Amarnes—didn't want an American nobody in love with their son. The country's heir. Of course, she hadn't realised that when she'd met Anders in a bar in Oslo; she'd thought he was just an ordinary person, or as ordinary as a man like him could be considered to be. Golden-haired, charming, with an effortless grace and confidence that had drawn her to his side with the irresistible force of a magnet. And even now, under Leo Christensen's sardonic scrutiny, she clung to that memory, to the knowledge that he loved her and she loved him. Except, where was he? Did he know his cousin was trying to bribe her?

Phoebe straightened and forced herself to meet Leo's scornful gaze directly. 'I'm afraid you don't have enough.'

Leo's mouth curled in something close to a smile, the smile of a snake. 'Try me.'

Rage coursed through her, clean and strong, fuelling her and overriding her fear. 'You don't have enough because there *isn't* enough, Mr Christensen—'

'Your Grace, actually,' Leo corrected softly. 'My formal title is the Duke of Larsvik.'

Phoebe swallowed at the reminder of just what kind of people she was dealing with. Powerful, rich. *Royal*. People who didn't want her…but Anders did. That, she resolved, would be enough. Plenty.

She'd had no idea when Anders asked her to meet his family that they actually comprised the king and queen of Amarnes, an island principality off the coast of Norway. And this man too, a man Phoebe recognised from his endless appearances in the tabloids, usually the lead player in some sordid drama involving women, cars, gambling, or all three. Anders had told her about Leo, had warned her, and after just a few minutes' conversation with Leo she believed everything he'd ever said.

'He's a bad influence, always has been. My family tried to reform him, they thought I could help. But no one can help Leo...'

And who was going to help *her*? Anders had told his parents about her last night; she hadn't been present. Clearly, Phoebe thought, swallowing a bubble of near-hysterical laughter, that conversation hadn't gone well. So they'd sent Leo, the black sheep, to deal with her...the problem.

She shook her head now, not wanting to speak Leo Christensen's damn title, not wanting him to know just how out of her depth she was. Yet he knew it; of course he did. She saw it in the scornful little smile he gave her, the way his gaze flicked over her in easy dismissal, making her feel like trash.

Still, if he knew it, at least that meant there was nothing to lose. She lifted her chin. 'Fine, Your *Grace*. But there's no amount of money you could give me that would make me leave Anders.' Brave words, she knew, and there was no way she'd take Leo's money, but still...where was Anders?

Leo stared at her for a moment, those sensual, sleepy eyes narrowing, flaring. His mouth twisted and he turned away. 'How quaint, my dear,' he murmured. 'How very ad-mirable. So it's true love?'

Humiliation and annoyance prickled along her skin,

chased up her spine. He made what she had with Anders sound so trite. So cheap. 'Yes, it is.'

Leo shoved his hands in his pockets and strolled to the window, gazing out at the plaza in front of Amarnes's royal palace. It was a brilliant summer morning, the sky blue with faint wisps of cloud, the jagged, violet mountains a stunning backdrop to the capital city of Njardvik's cluster of buildings, the bronze statues of Amarnes's twin eagles—the country's emblem— glinting in the sun. 'How long have you known my cousin?' he finally asked and Phoebe shifted her bag to her other shoulder.

'Ten days.'

He turned around, one eyebrow arched, his hands still in his pockets. His silence was eloquent, and Phoebe felt a blush stain her throat and rise to her cheeks. Ten days. It wasn't much; it sounded ridiculous. And yet she *knew*. She knew when Anders looked at her...and yet now this man was looking at her, his amber gaze sleepy and yet so sardonic, so knowing. Ten days. Ten days was nothing. And judging by the contemptuous curl of Leo's lip, he thought so too. Phoebe straightened. What did she care what Leo Christensen, the Playboy Prince of Amarnes, thought of her? He was a man given over to pleasure, vice. Yet, standing in front of him now, she was conscious of a darker streak in him, something more alarming and dangerous than the antics of a mere playboy. An emotion emanated from him, something dark and unknowable, yet a force to be reckoned with...if only she knew what it was.

'And you think ten days is long enough to know someone?' Leo asked in that honeyed voice that wound around Phoebe like a spell even as alarm prickled along her spine. 'To love him?' he pressed, his voice so soft, so seductively mild, yet still with that thread of darkness that Phoebe didn't understand. Didn't want to.

She shrugged, determined to stay defiant. She wasn't going to defend what she felt for Anders, or what he felt for her. She knew it would sound contrived, as trite and silly as Leo was determined to make it.

'You realise,' Leo continued in that same soft voice that made the hairs on the nape of Phoebe's neck prickle, 'that if he stays with you—marries you, as he has suggested—you will be queen? Something this country is not prepared to allow.'

'They won't have to,' Phoebe returned. The idea of her becoming queen was utterly terrifying. 'Anders told me he will abdicate.'

Leo's eyes narrowed, his body stilling. 'Abdicate?' he said softly. 'He said that?'

Phoebe jutted her chin. 'Yes.'

Leo's eyes met hers and he held her gaze with unrelenting hardness. 'Then he will never become king.'

She would not let this man make her feel guilty. 'He doesn't even want to be king—'

Leo let out a bark of disbelieving laughter. 'Doesn't want to be king? When it's all he's ever known?'

'He told me—'

He shrugged in derisive dismissal. 'Anders,' he said, cutting her off, 'rarely knows what he wants.'

'Well, he does now,' Phoebe returned with more determination than she felt at the moment. Somehow, as the target of Leo's incredulous scorn, she found her determination—her faith—trickling away. 'He wants me,' she said, and it came out sounding childish.

Leo stared at her for a moment, his expression turning thoughtful, then blank, ominously, dangerously neutral.

He could be thinking anything. Planning anything. He cocked his head. 'And you…want…him?'

'Of course I do.' Phoebe fidgeted again; the reception room with its heavy drapes and furniture felt oppressive. A gilded prison. Would she be allowed to walk out of here? She was conscious of her uncertain status as a foreigner in a small and fiercely independent country, and she was even more conscious of the man in front of her, a man with power and authority and clearly no compunction in using both for his own ends.

And where, oh, where was Anders? Did he know she'd been sent for? Why wasn't he looking for her? Since he'd announced their relationship to the royal family he'd been absent, and she now felt a treacherous flicker of doubt.

'You know him?' Leo pressed. 'Enough to live a life of exile?'

'Exile from a family that doesn't accept or love him,' Phoebe returned. 'Anders has never wanted this, Mr— Your Grace.' She swept an arm to encompass the room and the entire palace with its endless expectations.

'Oh, hasn't he?' Leo laughed once, a sharp, unpleasant sound. He moved back to the window, his back to her, seeming lost in thought. Phoebe waited, impatience and worse—fear—starting to fray her hope. Her faith.

'Would ten thousand dollars, American, do it?' Leo asked, his back to her, his voice musing. 'Or more like fifty?'

Phoebe straightened, glad for the renewed wave of outrage that poured through her, replacing the fear and doubt. 'I told you, no amount—'

'Phoebe.' Leo turned around, and the way he said her name sounded strangely gentle, although his eyes were hard, his expression remote. 'Do you honestly think a man like Anders can make you happy?'

'And how could a man like you possibly know?' Phoebe flung back, annoyed and angry that he was making her feel this way. Making her wonder.

Leo stiffened, his face blanking once more. 'A man like me?' he enquired with stiff politeness.

'Anders has told me about you,' Phoebe said, both the fear and the anger spiking her words, making them hurt, making her want to hurt him—although how could you hurt a man like Leo Christensen? A man who had seen it all, done it all and cared about nothing? Or so the newspapers said, Anders said, and the man in front of her with his sardonic smile and cold voice seemed to confirm every awful thing she'd ever heard. 'You know nothing about love or loyalty,' she continued. 'You care only about your own pleasure—and I suppose I'm a little inconvenience to that—'

'That you are,' Leo cut her off. For a second Phoebe wondered if she'd hurt him with her words. No, impossible. He was actually smiling, his mouth curving in a way that was really most unpleasant. Frightening. 'Quite an inconvenience, Miss Wells. You have no idea just how much.' As if drawing a mask over the first one, Leo's expression changed. It became sleepy, speculative, his smile turning seductive. He took a step closer to her. 'What would have happened, do you suppose,' he asked in that soft, bedroom voice, 'if you'd met me first?'

'Nothing,' Phoebe snapped, but even so her heart rate kicked up a notch as Leo kept walking towards her with languorous, knowing ease, stopping only a hairsbreadth away. She could feel his heat, smell the faint woodsy tang of his aftershave. She stared determinedly at his shirt, refusing to be intimidated, to show how afraid—how affected—she was. Yet even so, her gaze helplessly moved upwards from the buttons of his fine silk shirt to where they were undone, to that brown column of his throat where a pulse leaped and jerked, and Phoebe felt an answering response deep inside, a tug in her belly that could only be called yearning. Desire.

She flushed in shame.

Leo gave a low chuckle. He raised one hand to brush a wayward curl from her forehead, and Phoebe jerked instinctively in response, felt the heat of his fingers against her skin.

'Are you so sure about that?' he queried softly.

'Yes...'

Yet at that moment she wasn't, and they both knew it. Heard it in her ragged breathing, saw it in how she almost swayed towards him. Horrible man, Phoebe thought savagely, yet she condemned herself as well. She shouldn't let him affect her like this, not if she loved Anders, which she did.

Didn't she?

'So sure,' Leo whispered, his voice a soft sneer, and his hand dropped from her forehead to her throat, where her pulse beat as frantically as a trapped bird's. With one finger he gently touched that sensitive hollow, causing Phoebe to gasp aloud in what—? Shock? Outrage?

Pleasure?

She could still feel the reverberation of his touch, as if a string had been plucked in her soul, and the single note of seduction played throughout her body.

'Phoebe!'

Gasping again, this time in relief, Phoebe stumbled away from Leo, from his knowing smile and hands. She turned towards the doorway and saw Anders, appearing like the golden god Baldur from the Norse myth, smiling at Phoebe with a radiant certainty that dispelled all her own fears like the dawn mist over the mountains. 'I've been looking for you. No one would tell me where you were—'

'I've been here—' tears of relief stung Phoebe's eyes as she hurried towards him '—with your cousin.'

Anders glanced at Leo, and his expression darkened with a deeper emotion. Phoebe couldn't tell if it was disapproval or fear or perhaps even jealousy. She swallowed and glanced at Leo. She saw with a sharp jolt of shock that he was staring at his cousin with a bland expression that somehow still managed to convey a deep and unwavering coldness. *Hatred.* And Phoebe was reminded of the ending of the Norse myth she'd read about during her travels through Scandinavia: that Baldur had been murdered by his twin brother, Hod, the god of darkness and winter.

'What do you want with Phoebe, Leo?' Anders demanded, and his voice sounded strained, even petulant.

'Nothing.' Leo smiled, shrugged, spreading his hands wide in a universal gesture of innocence. 'She obviously loves you, Anders.' His mouth twisted in a smile that didn't look quite right.

'She does,' Anders agreed, putting an arm around Phoebe's shoulder. She leaned against him, grateful for his strength, yet still conscious of Leo's dark, unwavering gaze. 'I don't know why you were talking to her, Leo, but we're both determined to be together—'

'And such determination is so very admirable,' Leo cut across him softly. 'I will tell the king so.'

Anders's expression hardened, his lower lip jutting out in an expression more appropriate to a six-year-old before he shrugged and nodded. 'You may do so. If he wanted you to convince me otherwise…'

Leo smiled and that simple gesture made Phoebe want

to shiver. There was nothing kind or good or loving about it. 'Obviously, I cannot.' He lifted one shoulder. 'What more is there to say?'

'Nothing,' Anders finished. He turned to Phoebe. 'It's time for us to leave, Phoebe. There's nothing for us here. We can take the ferry to Oslo and then catch the afternoon train to Paris.'

Phoebe nodded, relieved, knowing she should be excited. Ecstatic.

Yet as she walked from the room, Anders's arm still around her shoulders, she was conscious only of Leo's unrelenting gaze, and that dark emotion emanating from him which seemed strangely—impossibly—like sorrow.

CHAPTER TWO

Six years later

IT WAS raining in Paris, a needling grey drizzle that blanketed the royal mourners in grey, and made the images on the television screen blurry and virtually unrecognisable.

Not, Phoebe acknowledged, that she'd met any of Anders's family besides his cousin. Leo. Even now his name made her skin prickle, made her recall that terrible, cold look he'd given Anders as they'd left the Amarnesian palace. That was the last time either she or Anders had seen any of his family, or even stepped foot in his native country.

Six years ago…a lifetime, or two. Certainly more than one life had been affected—formed, changed—in the last half-decade.

'Mommy?' Christian stood behind the sofa where Phoebe had curled up, watching the funeral on one of those obscure cable channels. Now she turned to smile at her five-year-old son, who was gazing at the television with a faint frown. 'What are you watching?'

'Just…' Phoebe shrugged, reaching to turn off the television. How to explain to Christian that his father—the father he hadn't ever even seen—had died? It would be meaningless to Christian, who had long ago accepted the fact that he didn't have a daddy. He didn't need one, had been happy with the life Phoebe had provided, with friends and relatives and school here in New York.

'Just what?' Christian put his hands on his hips, his expression halfway between a pout and a mischievous grin. He was all boy, curious about everything, always asking what, why, who.

'Watching something,' Phoebe murmured. She rose from the sofa, giving her son a quick one-armed hug. 'Isn't it time for dinner?' Smiling, she pulled him along, tousling his hair, into the kitchen of their Greenwich Village apartment. Outside the sunlight slanted across Washington Square, filling the space with golden light.

Yet as she pulled pots and pans from the cupboards, mindlessly listening to Christian talk about his latest craze—some kind of superhero, or were they super-robots? Pheobe could never keep them straight—her mind slipped back to the blurry image of the funeral on television.

Anders, her husband of exactly one month, was dead. She shook her head, unable to summon more than a sense of sorrowful pity for a man who had swept into her life and out again with equal abruptness. It hadn't taken very long for Anders to realise Phoebe had been nothing more than a passing fancy, and Phoebe had understood with equal speed how shallow and spoiled Anders really was. Yet at least that brief period of folly had given her something wonderful…Christian.

'I like the green ones best…' Christian tugged on her sleeve. 'Mom, are you listening?'

'Sorry, honey.' Phoebe smiled down at Christian in

apology even as she noticed that she'd let the water for the pasta boil dry. She had to get her mind out of the past. She hadn't thought about Anders for years, and sometimes it felt as though that short, regrettable episode had never occurred. Yet his death had brought old memories to the surface—namely, that horrible interview at the palace. Even now Pheobe remembered the look in Leo Christensen's eyes, the way he'd touched her…and the way she'd responded.

With a jolt Phoebe realised she was remembering Leo, not Anders. Anders had receded into her memory as nothing more than a faded, blurry image, like an old photograph, yet Leo…Leo she remembered as sharply and clearly as if he were standing right in front of her.

She glanced around the sunny kitchenette of her modest but comfortable apartment, almost as if she would see Leo standing darkly in the shadows. She gave a little laugh at her own ridiculous behaviour. Leo Christensen—all the Christensens, that entire life—was thousands of miles away. She and Anders had quietly separated just months after Leo had offered her fifty thousand dollars to leave him, and she'd never seen any of them again. She'd moved to New York with Christian, started over with the support of friends and family, and relegated the incident to a dark, unswept corner of her mind…that now felt the bright, glaring light of day.

Abruptly Phoebe turned off the stove. 'How about pizza?' she asked Christian brightly, who responded with a delighted smile.

'Angelo's?' he asked hopefully, naming their favourite neighbourhood pizza joint, and Phoebe nodded.

'Absolutely.'

Phoebe went to get their coats, only to stop in uneasy

surprise at the sight of Christian in front of the television once more. He'd turned it back on and was watching the funeral procession, tracking the coffin's progression down one of Paris's main thoroughfares, the flag's twin eagles with their austere, noble profiles visible even in the gloom. 'Is that man dead?'

Phoebe swallowed, a pang of sorrow for Anders's wasted life piercing her. 'Yes, it's a funeral.'

'Why is it on television?' Christian asked with his usual wide-eyed curiosity.

'Because he was a prince.'

'A prince?' Christian sounded moderately impressed. As a New Yorker, he encountered people of all walks of life every day. 'A real one?' he asked with a faint note of scepticism.

Phoebe almost smiled. 'Yes, a real one.' She wasn't about to explain to Christian about Anders's abdication or exile, or the fact that he was his father. She'd always intended for Christian to know the truth of his birth, but not like this, with a grainy image of a funeral on TV. Besides, Christian knew what was important: that Phoebe had wanted him and loved him. Nothing else needed matter.

With decisive determination she turned the TV off, the words of the French commentator fading away into silence.

'*Crown Prince of Amarnes...inebriated...reckless driving...his companion, a French model, died instantly along with him...*'

'Come on, scout,' she said lightly. 'Pizza time.'

They'd almost reached the door, almost missed them completely, Phoebe thought later, when she heard the knock.

Christian's eyes widened and they stared at each other, the only sound the awful, silent reverberation of the knock. Strange, Phoebe thought, how they both knew that knock was different. Three short, hard raps on the door, so unlike the flurry of light taps their neighbour, old Mrs Simpson, would give, along with a cheery hello.

Those short, sharp knocks which felt like a warning, a herald of nothing good, and somehow they both knew it. Phoebe felt that knowledge settle coldly in her bones, even as she wondered who—what—why. Just like Christian, she was filled with questions.

'Who could that be?' she murmured, trying to smile. Christian raced towards the door.

'I'll get it—'

'*No.*' Phoebe pushed past her son, flinging one arm out to bar Christian's way. 'Never answer to strangers, Christian.'

Taking a deep breath, Phoebe opened the door, and her heart sank at the two dark-suited men standing there. They had the bland good looks and ominously neutral expressions of government agents. In fact, it was men just like these who had summoned her to the palace all those years ago, ushered her into the room with Leo and his abominable offer of a pay-off.

'*How about fifty?*'

Phoebe pushed the memory away and stared at the two men filling up her doorway, trying to frame a thought. A rebuke.

'Madame Christensen?'

It was a name Phoebe hadn't heard in a long while; she'd reverted to her maiden name when she separated from Anders. Yet the presence of these men and the sound of her married name made the years fall away and suddenly she was back in Amarnes, facing Leo…

'*Are you so sure about that?*'

Even now she could remember—*feel*—how Leo had trailed his finger along her cheek, then lower to the V between her breasts, and she'd let him. Even now, across all the years, she remembered the inescapable fascination she'd had with him in those few brief moments, her body betraying her so quickly and easily.

Phoebe lifted her chin and met the blank face of one of the men. 'Actually my name is Ms Wells.'

The man stuck out his hand, which Phoebe took after a second's hesitation and then dropped almost immediately; her own hand was clammy and cold. 'My name is Erik Jensen. We are representatives of His Majesty, King Nicholas of Amarnes. Would you please come with us?'

'Mommy…' Christian's voice sounded strangled, and when Phoebe glanced back she saw her son's face was bleached white, his eyes huge and shocked. She felt the mirror of that expression on her own face, remembering how men like this had showed up in her grotty hostel, said nearly the exact same words. Six years ago she'd been too young, too bewildered and overwhelmed to do anything but acquiesce. Now she was older, harder, tougher. She knew better.

'I'm not going anywhere.'

Something flickered in the agent's face and Phoebe thought for a second it looked like pity. Fear crawled along her spine and up her throat.

'Madame Christensen—'

'Who is that?' Christian's voice sounded petulant and afraid, his hands clenched into fists at his sides. 'Why are you calling my mom that name?'

'I'm sorry.' Erik Jensen smiled briefly at the boy. 'Ms Wells.' He turned back to Phoebe. 'It would be better,' he said quietly, 'if you came. There is a representative waiting at the Amarnesian Consulate, to discuss—'

'I hardly think there is anything to discuss,' Phoebe replied coolly. 'In fact,' she continued, her voice a little stronger now, 'I think any necessary discussions were concluded six years ago.' When she and Anders had left the palace in a shroud of disapproval. He'd signed the papers of abdication, releasing him from the burden of the throne. Not one family member had said a word or seen them out. They'd slipped like shadows from the palace, unseen, forgotten. Except, perhaps, by Leo, with his cold, unwavering stare that still chilled her all these years later.

'Matters have changed,' Erik replied in that same neutral yet implacable tone. 'A discussion is necessary.'

Coldness seeped through her, swirled through her brain. *Matters have changed.* Such an innocuous yet ominous phrase. She felt Christian inch closer to her, his fingers curling around her leg. She felt his fear like a palpable force, and it angered her that these men could just come in here and in a matter of minutes—seconds—try to change her life. Order it around. 'Just a minute,' she told the agents stiffly, and turned back to the kitchen, Christian at her side.

'Mommy—' Christian tugged at her leg '—who are those men? Why are they so...' he paused, his voice trembling '...so scary?'

'They don't mean to be,' Phoebe said before she thought *I'll be damned if I apologise for them.* 'Anyway, I'm not scared of them.' She tried to smile, although like her son she felt the fear, crawling, insidious.

Why were those men here? What did they want?

She took a deep breath, forcing herself to think calmly. Coolly. Undoubtedly they wanted her to sign some paper, relinquishing her rights to Anders's money. He'd obviously had a lot of it, even though in their few weeks together he'd squandered his stipend with shocking ease. His father, King Nicholas, had insisted on his son's abdication, yet he'd still kept him well provided for with what mattered—champagne and women.

There was no reason to panic, to be afraid. Yet even as Phoebe told herself this, she felt the fear creep in and wind around her heart. She knew how much power the royal family had. Or, rather, she didn't know, couldn't fathom it, and that was what scared her. They were capable of so much. She'd seen it in the way they'd cut Anders out of the royal family as ruthlessly as if wielding scissors. She'd felt it in Leo's cold stare.

'Mommy—'

'I can't explain it all now, Christian.' Phoebe smiled down at her son, 'but I don't want you to be afraid. These men have a little business with me, and I need to deal with it. You can stay with Mrs Simpson for a little while, can't you?'

Christian wrinkled his nose. 'Her place smells like cats. And I want to stay with you.'

'I know, but…' Mindlessly Phoebe stroked Christian's hair, still soft as a baby's. Like the little boy he was, he jerked and squirmed away. 'All right,' she relented. Perhaps it was better if Christian stayed with her. 'You can come.' She tried to smile again, and managed it better. She felt her calm return, her sense of perspective. She didn't need to panic or fear. She'd built a life for herself here, felt it shining and strong all around her, and took courage from that knowledge. The past receded once more, as it was meant to do, as she needed it to.

A few minutes, perhaps an hour at the Amarnesian

Consulate, and this would all be forgotten. Her life would go on as planned.

She linked hands with Christian, and it was a sign of his nervousness that he let her. Resolutely she turned back to the government agents standing in the doorway like overgrown crows.

'I'll just gather a few things, and then we can be on our way.' She took another breath, injected a certain firmness into her voice. 'I'd like to resolve whatever discussion is necessary as soon as possible, and be home for dinner.'

Their silence, Phoebe reflected, was both ominous and eloquent.

It only took a few minutes to pack a bag with a few snacks and toys for Christian, and then she followed the men down the narrow stairs to the street. Mrs Simpson, in a frayed dressing gown and carpet slippers, poked her head out as they descended, her expression curious and a little worried.

'Phoebe, is everything all right?' she called, and Phoebe's voice sounded rusty as she cleared her throat and replied as cheerfully as she could,

'Yes, fine.' She tried a smile, but felt it slide right off her face. She turned away, clutching Christian to her, and willed her racing heart to slow.

A sedan that screamed discretion with its tinted windows and government plates idled at the kerb, and another dark-suited agent exited the car with smooth assurance and ushered Phoebe and Christian into the back.

As she slid into the soft leather interior and heard the door's lock click into place, she wondered if she was making the biggest mistake of her life, or just being melodramatic.

She'd sign a paper, she'd relinquish whatever rights to

money that they wanted, and then she'd go home, she repeated to herself in a desperate litany. And, Phoebe added grimly, forget this had ever happened.

The sun was setting, sending long, golden rays over the mellow brick townhouses and tenements of Greenwich Village as the sedan purred through the neighbourhood's narrow streets, the pavement cafés and funky boutiques possessing only a scattering of patrons on this chilly November day.

Christian sat close to her side, his expression closed yet alert. Phoebe felt a sharp pang of pride at the way he composed himself. He knew she was feeling as afraid as she was...except she was determined not to be afraid.

That time had passed.

She turned towards the window and watched as the narrow streets of the Village gave way to the wider stretch of Broadway, and then, as they headed uptown on First Avenue, to the broad expanse of the United Nations concourse. Finally the sedan pulled onto a narrow side street wreathed with the flags of various consulates, stopping in front of an elegant townhouse with steep stairs and a wrought-iron railing.

Phoebe slipped out of the car, still holding Christian's hand, and followed the agents into the Armanesian Consulate. Inside it felt like a home, an upscale one, with silk curtains at the windows and priceless, polished antiques decorating the foyer. Phoebe's footsteps were silenced by the thick Aubusson carpet.

As they entered, a woman in a dark suit—was it actually a uniform for these people?—her blonde hair cut in a professional bob, started forward.

'Madame Christensen,' she murmured. 'You are expected.' She glanced at Christian, who clenched Phoebe's hand more tightly. 'I can take the child—'

Phoebe stiffened at the words. 'No one is taking my son.'

The woman flushed, embarrassed and confused, and glanced at Erik Jensen, who hovered at Phoebe's shoulder.

'There is a room upstairs, with every comfort,' he said quietly. 'Toys, books, a television.' He paused diplomatically. 'Perhaps it would be better…'

Phoebe bit her lip. She should have insisted on leaving Christian with Mrs. Simpson and spared him this. Yet she hadn't wanted to be parted with him then, and she didn't now. Even more so she didn't want Christian to witness any unpleasant altercations with some palace official determined on making sure she received nothing from Anders's death.

'All right,' she relented, 'but I want him brought back down to me in fifteen minutes.'

Jensen gave a little shrug of assent, and Phoebe turned to Christian. 'Will you be…?'

Her little boy straightened, throwing his shoulders back. 'I'll be fine,' he said, and his bravery made her eyes sting.

She watched as he followed the dark-suited woman up the ornately curving stairs before turning resolutely to follow Jensen into one of the consulate private reception rooms.

'You may wait here,' he told her as Phoebe prowled through the elegantly appointed room, taking in the gloomy portraits, the polished furniture, the Amarnesian insignia on everything from the coasters to the curtains. 'Would you like a coffee? Tea?'

'No, thank you,' she said, resisting the urge to wrap her arms around herself even though the room wasn't cold. Far from it—it was stuffy, hot. Oppressive. 'I'd just like to get on with it, please, and go home.'

Jensen nodded and withdrew, and Phoebe was alone.

She glanced around the room, a gilded prison. This was so much like the last time she'd been summoned to the royal family—had she learned nothing in six years? She'd let herself be bullied then; she wouldn't now. She didn't want Anders's money, she didn't want anything from him that he hadn't been prepared to give her when he was alive, and she acknowledged grimly just how much that had been: nothing.

Nothing then, nothing now. And that was fine, because she was fine. She'd sign their damn paper and go home.

She registered the soft click of the door opening and stiffened, suddenly afraid to turn around and face the person waiting for her there.

For in that moment she knew—just as she had known when she'd heard those three short raps on the door of her apartment—her life was about to change. Impossibly, irrevocably. For ever.

For she knew from the coldness in her bones, the leaden weight of her numbed heart, that a fussy palace official or consulate pencil-pusher was not waiting for her across ten yards of opulence. She knew, even before turning, who was waiting. Who had been sent to deal with her—an inconvenience, an embarrassment—again.

She turned slowly, her heart beginning a slow yet relentless hammering, a distant part of her still hoping that he wouldn't be there—that after all these years it couldn't be him—

But it was. Of course it was. Standing in the doorway, a faint, sardonic smile on his face and glittering in his eyes, was Leo Christensen.

CHAPTER THREE

'WHAT...?' The single word came out involuntarily, a gasp of shock and fear as the sight of Leo standing there so calm and assured brought the memories flooding back. Phoebe threw her shoulders back and lifted her chin. 'What are you doing here?' she asked in a calmer voice.

Leo arched an eyebrow as he strolled into the room, closing the door softly behind him. 'Is this not the Amarnesian Consulate?' he asked, and Phoebe was conscious of how effortlessly he made her feel like an interloper. An ignorant one.

'Then I suppose the question to ask,' she replied coldly, 'is why *I* am here.'

'Indeed, that is an interesting question,' Leo murmured, his voice as soft and dangerous as it had been six years ago. Phoebe felt it wrap around her with its seductive chill and tried not to shiver.

He was the same, she thought numbly, the same as he'd always been. The same sleepy, bedroom eyes, the same aura of confident sensuality even dressed as he was in a dark suit, undoubtedly coming as he did from Anders's funeral, although there was no sign of grief in his saturnine features.

'How did you get here?' Phoebe blurted. 'You were in Paris, at the funeral—'

'I was this morning,' Leo agreed blandly. 'Then I flew here.'

She tried for a laugh. 'Am I that important?'

'No,' Leo replied, and turned from her to move to a small table equipped with a few crystal decanters and glasses. 'May I offer you a drink? Sherry, brandy?'

'I don't want a drink,' Phoebe replied through gritted teeth. 'I want to know why I'm here and then go home.'

'Home,' Leo repeated musingly. He poured a snifter of brandy, the liquid glinting gold in the lamplight. 'And where is that, precisely?'

'My apartment—'

'A one-bedroom in a rather run-down tenement—'

Phoebe stiffened, thinking of the rather astronomical rent she paid for an apartment most people would think more than adequate. 'Obviously your opinion of what constitutes run-down differs from mine.' She met his gaze directly, refusing to flinch. 'I'm not sure what the point of this is,' she continued. 'I assume I was summoned here for a purpose, to sign some paper—'

'A paper?' Leo asked. He sounded politely curious. 'What kind of paper?' He smiled slightly, and that faint little gesture chilled her all the more. Leo's smiles were worse than his scowls or sneers; there was something cold and feral about them, and it made her think—remember— that he was capable of anything. She'd read it in the tabloids' smear stories; she'd felt it the last time she'd stood across from him and listened to him try to bribe her, and she'd seen it in the cold, cold look he'd given Anders.

'Some kind of paper,' she repeated with a defensive shrug. 'Signing away any rights to Anders's money—'

'Anders's money?' Leo sounded almost amused now. 'Had he any money?'

'He certainly seemed to spend it.' Phoebe heard the ring of bitterness in her voice and flinched at what it revealed.

'Ah. Yes. He *spent* money, but it wasn't his. It belonged to his father, King Nicholas.' Leo took a sip of his brandy. 'Actually, Anders hadn't a euro or cent or whatever currency you prefer to his name. He was really quite, quite broke.'

His words seemed to fall into the empty space of the room, reverberate in the oppressive silence. 'I see,' Phoebe finally managed, but sadly, scarily, she didn't. If Anders didn't have any money…then why was she here? 'Then is it about the Press?' she asked. *Hoped.* 'A gagging order or some such? So I don't write some sort of embarrassing memoir?'

Leo's smile widened; he really was genuinely amused now, and it made Phoebe feel ignorant again. Stupid. 'Have you memoirs?' he queried. 'And would they be so…embarrassing?'

Phoebe felt herself flush, and she shrugged, angry now. Angry and afraid. Not a good combination. 'Then just tell me why I am here…*Your Grace.*'

The smile vanished from Leo's face before he corrected with lethal softness, 'Actually, my title is now Your Highness. Since Anders abdicated, I am the country's heir.'

Phoebe stilled, the realisation trickling coldly through her. She hadn't realised Leo was now the crown prince, although of course she should have known. She knew there was no one else. Anders and Leo were both only children, which was why they'd been raised like brothers.

For a second the old myth flashed through Phoebe's

mind as it had the last time she'd seen Leo: Hod and
Baldur. Twins, one dark, one light. One good, one evil.
Except she knew Anders's true colours now, and he was
far from being good or light. Not evil perhaps, but silly,
shallow, selfish and vain. She shook her head, banishing
the memories. 'Your Highness, then. What do you want
with me? Because I'd prefer to get to the point and go
home. My son is waiting upstairs and he's hungry.' Brave
words, she knew. Strong words, but she didn't feel particu-
larly brave or strong. The longer she remained in Leo's
company, bearing the weight of his silence, the more she
felt her strength being tested. Sapped. 'Well?' she snapped,
hating the way he was toying with her, sipping his brandy
and watching her over the rim of his glass as if she was an
object of amusement or worse, pity.

'I don't want anything with you in particular,' Leo
replied coolly. 'However, my uncle, King Nicholas, hasn't
been well, and he has suffered great regret over what
happened with Anders—'

'You mean forcing his son to abdicate? To leave his
country in disgrace?' Phoebe filled in.

Leo smiled over the rim of his glass. 'As I recall, you
told me Anders didn't even want to be king.'

Phoebe coloured, discomfited that he remembered the
particulars of their conversation six years ago…as did she.

'He didn't,' she mumbled, turning away to gaze unsee-
ingly out of the embassy window. Outside, night had
fallen, and a passing taxi washed the room in pale yellow
light before streaming onwards into the darkness. Phoebe
was suddenly conscious of how long she'd been in this
room with Leo, and she turned around. 'I want to see my
son.'

Something flickered across his face—what?—but then

he gave a tiny shrug. 'Of course. He's upstairs, quite happy, but I'll have Nora bring him down as soon as we've concluded our conversation.'

'And what more is there to say?' Phoebe demanded. 'I'm sorry King Nicholas regrets what happened, but the past is the past and can't be changed. And frankly none of it has anything to do with me.'

'Doesn't it?' Leo queried softly, so softly, and yet it felt as if he'd dropped a handful of ice cubes down her back, or even straight into her soul. Those two little words were spoken with such confidence, such arrogance and power and knowledge, and suddenly, desperately, Phoebe wished she'd never agreed to come to the consulate. Wished, almost, that she'd never met Anders—she'd certainly wished that before—except for the saving grace of Christian.

Still, even under the onslaught of Leo's dark, knowing gaze, those sleepy, bedroom eyes with the long lashes and golden irises now flared with awareness, with knowledge, she forced herself to continue. 'No, it doesn't. In fact, you most likely know that I haven't even seen Anders in years. We separated a month after we married, *Your Highness*, and were practically divorced—'

'Practically?' Leo interrupted. 'Had you consulted with a solicitor? Filed papers?'

Phoebe felt yet another telltale blush staining her cheeks with damning colour even as an inexplicable dread settled coldly in her stomach. 'No, I hadn't, but...' She stopped, suddenly, the silence worse than any words she could say, explanations—excuses—she could give.

'But?' Leo filled in, his eyes, nearly the same colour as the brandy in the glass he held, glittering for a moment with—what? Mockery? Contempt? *Anger?* 'Couldn't bear to make that final cut?' he continued in that awful, soft voice. 'Couldn't stand to walk away from a man like Anders?' He took a step closer to her and Phoebe found she couldn't move. She was mesmerised, strangely drawn by his words and yet chilled too by that unfathomable darkness in his eyes and voice, that depth of some unknowable emotion she'd sensed in him at their first meeting. Leo took another step, and then another, so he was standing only a few inches away, and she was reminded forcefully of when he'd stood so close to her before, when his fingers had brushed her in that faint, damning caress and he'd asked her, '*What would have happened...if you'd met me first?*' Now he asked another mocking question. 'Were you hoping he'd come back to you, Phoebe?'

Phoebe blinked, forced herself to react. His assessment was so far from the truth, and yet the truth was something she could not bring herself to tell. She stepped away and drew a breath. 'No, I most certainly was not. And whether Anders and I divorced or even considered divorcing is of no concern to you—'

'Actually,' Leo corrected, taking a sip of his brandy, 'it is.' He watched, smiling faintly, enjoying her shock and discomfiture. Phoebe felt her hands curl into fists, her nails biting into her palms. She knew Leo was waiting for her to ask why, and she didn't want to. Didn't want to know.

'It wasn't anyone's concern whether we married or not,' she finally said, striving to keep her voice cool, 'so I hardly see why it matters if we divorced or not.' She drew herself up, throwing her shoulders back. 'Now frankly I've had enough of these power games, Your Highness. You may find it amusing to keep me here like a mouse with a cat, but my son is undoubtedly unsettled and afraid and I have nothing more to say to you or anyone from Amarnes. So—'

'Oh, Phoebe.' Leo shook his head, and for a moment Phoebe thought he genuinely felt sorry for her, and that realisation scared her more than anything else.

'Don't call me—'

'Your name? But we are relatives, of a sort.'

'Of a sort,' Phoebe agreed coldly. 'The sort that have nothing to do with each other.'

'That,' Leo informed her, setting his glass down in a careful, deliberate movement, 'is about to change.'

He was trying to scare her, Phoebe decided. Hoped, even. It was about power, about Leo feeling as if he was in control, and she wouldn't let him. He might be a prince, he might have all the money and power and knowledge, but she had her courage and her child. She had her memories, her own knowledge of how the last six years had shaped and strengthened her, and she wouldn't back down now, especially not to Leo. He'd intimidated and bullied her before; she wouldn't let him now.

'Why don't you just spit it out, Leo,' she asked, glad her voice matched his own for strength, 'instead of giving me all these insidious little hints? Are you trying to frighten me? Because it's not working.' Well, it was, a bit, but she wasn't about to tell him that. Leo merely arched an eyebrow, and Phoebe continued, her voice raw, demanding, and a little desperate. 'What do you want? Why did your damn agents bring me here?'

'Because the king wishes it,' Leo replied simply. He gave her a little smile, and Phoebe pressed a fist to her lips before dropping it.

'What do you mean?'

'I told you, King Nicholas regrets his separation from

Anders. I suppose he always did, but he didn't realise it until too late.' Leo's lips twisted in something close to a smile, and Phoebe wondered what kind of man could actually smile at such a moment, at the explanation of such a futile tragedy. Well, she knew the answer...a man like Leo.

'I'm sorry for your uncle's loss,' she finally said, keeping her voice stiff with dignity. 'For everyone's. But as I said before, it has little to do with me.'

'But you see,' Leo countered softly, 'it does. Or perhaps not with you, but at least with your son.' He paused, his words seeming to echo in the oppressive heaviness of the room, of the moment. 'The king's grandchild.'

Phoebe did not reply. She couldn't think of anything to say, to think, so she turned away to the window once more, as if she could find answers there. She blinked, trying to focus on the shapes of passing cars, but she couldn't see. Everything was blurred, and for a second she thought it was because of the rain. Then she realised it was because of the tears clouding her vision.

She took a breath, willed the tears to recede, to feel strong again. The last thing she wanted was for Leo to see her weakness, for surely if he was aware of it, he would use it.

Yet standing there, the lump of emotion still lodged in her throat, she realised she wasn't even very surprised. Of course the royal family of Amarnes wouldn't leave her alone. Leave Christian alone. For while they may have professed no interest in her son while Anders was alive, now that he was dead...?

Her child was all they had of him. And that was what she had to remember, Phoebe told herself, stiffening her shoulders, her spine. He was *her* child...in every way that mattered.

She swallowed again, meaning to turn to face Leo, but suddenly he was there, his presence behind her, like a looming shadow. It was an unwelcome surprise, as was the hand that rested briefly, heavily on her shoulder, the warmth of his fingers burning her even through the layers of her sweater and coat.

'I'm sorry.'

It was the last thing she expected, the words, and, even more so, the raw compassion underneath them. She didn't trust it, didn't allow herself to. How could she? She'd trusted Anders, she wasn't about to trust his cousin, and most of all she wasn't about to trust herself, as much as she wanted to. For in that moment she wanted to believe Leo was sorry, she wanted to believe he could be—what? A *friend*?

The idea was so laughable as to be offensive. Phoebe turned around, shrugging Leo's hand off her shoulder, and he stepped away, his expression bland once more.

'What exactly are you sorry for, Leo?' she asked coolly. 'Bringing me here? Upsetting my son? Thinking you have some kind of control over me just because you're a prince?'

Leo shrugged, his tone matching hers. 'None of the above. I'm sorry because you obviously loved Anders, and now he's dead.'

It was such a flat, matter-of-fact statement; it hardly could be called a condolence. Phoebe inclined her head in acknowledgement.

'Thank you. But anything I felt for Anders ended six years ago. I'm sorry he died in such a tragic way, but…' She drew in a breath. 'What I had with him is far, far in the past. I have a life here now, and so does Christian, regardless of what the king of Amarnes thinks or feels. He has not tried to contact us once in the last six years. What is my son to think, to learn he suddenly has a grandfather who cared nothing for him before?'

'I imagine he'd be grateful to learn he has some family,' Leo replied, his tone still cool.

'He has my mother—'

'On his father's side. But you've never even told Christian about Anders, have you? He doesn't even know that his father is—was—a prince.'

'And why should he?' Phoebe flashed. 'Anders abdicated the throne and had no interest in being a father to Christian. We're far better here in New York with our friends and family. My mother has been a doting grandmother to Christian, and he's wanted for nothing.'

Leo merely arched one eyebrow in silent scepticism, making Phoebe fume. 'You don't need to live in a palace or ride in a Rolls-Royce to be considered cared for, you know,' she snapped. 'Christian has had a perfectly acceptable and happy childhood—'

'He is the son of a prince, descended from royalty,' Leo said quietly. 'And you don't think he should know?'

'None of you wanted to know,' Phoebe returned. 'Not once—'

'Ah, but you see, we didn't know about Christian,' Leo told her softly. 'By the time he'd made an appearance, you'd already separated from Anders—or should I say he separated from you? Either way, you disappeared from his life. And the royal family had no interest in you...until we learned you had a child. How old is he, Phoebe? Five, six?'

'Five.' Almost six, but she wasn't about to tell that to Leo. Let him draw whatever conclusions he wanted.

Leo paused, took a step closer. 'You must have fallen

pregnant right away. Or did it happen after he left you? You were together for how long? A few weeks?'

'A little over a month,' she answered tightly.

'What happened, Phoebe?' Leo asked, his voice as soft as a caress. 'Did Anders smile and say sorry as he always did? Did he make it up to you?' Another step and she could feel his breath on her cheek, felt his hand touch her shoulder, trailing his fingers, and even now she felt a sharp, unwanted pang of need—desire—at the simple touch. She shrugged away. 'Is that how Christian came about?'

'It's absolutely no concern of yours,' she said coldly. The last thing she wanted Leo to know was the truth of Christian's birth. Let him believe she'd, however briefly, made up with Anders. The idea was repellent, but so was the alternative…Leo knowing the truth.

'Perhaps not,' Leo agreed, 'but the fact remains that Christian is my concern, or at least my uncle, the king's.'

'*No.*' The word was torn from her, and Phoebe turned to see Leo looking at her again with a strange compassion that rested oddly on the harshly beautiful features of his face. She wasn't used to seeing a gentler emotion softening his mouth, lighting his eyes. She didn't like it and she didn't trust it.

'Yes,' he corrected her softly, spreading his hands for a moment before dropping them again, 'and I'm afraid there's nothing you can do about it.'

The words buzzed like flies in Phoebe's brain and she tasted bile. She wasn't ready for this, she realised. She didn't have the strength for a second round with Leo. She drew in a shaky breath. 'I'd like to check on Christian,' she said, and was glad her voice was steady. 'Alone. And then we can continue this conversation.'

Something sparked in Leo's eyes, something almost

like admiration or at least a certain grudging respect, and he inclined his head. 'Very well.' He moved to the door and pressed an unseen button. Within seconds a dark-suited official entered almost soundlessly. Leo spoke to the official in Danish, and Phoebe could only make out a few words.

'Sven will take you upstairs,' Leo told her. 'When you are satisfied Christian is comfortable, we will continue.'

Phoebe nodded, turning to follow Sven. Leo had turned his back on her and was pouring himself another drink, staring out at the black night as if he too was seeking answers in the darkness.

The door clicked softly shut behind him and Leo took a strong swallow of his drink, the alcohol burning all the way to his gut. He needed the sensation, the sedation from feeling. Remembering.

Regretting.

Anders was dead. That was enough to damn him. Dead. A wasted, reckless life, and not once had Leo tried to rein him in, teach him control. No, that hadn't been his job. His job, Leo acknowledged sourly, had been to stay out of the way, to be the unneeded spare, and of course to keep Anders happy. Entertained.

It hadn't been very much of a job.

Even now Leo remembered the slow burn of constant dismissals and rejection. Stay out of the way, Leo. Be quiet and do what you're told. Do not anger the king… His mother's pleas, the desperate attempts of a woman who had been cast off by the royal family as soon as she'd been made a widow. She hadn't wanted the same fate for Leo.

So his fate—his duty—had been to exist as Anders's

older shadow. He'd accompanied his cousin on his escapades and he'd enjoyed them himself and now...

Now those days were over, and his duty lay elsewhere.

Leo turned away from the window, impatient with his own maudlin reflections. He thought of Phoebe, felt a flicker of reluctant admiration for her strength and courage, even though she was clearly shocked by Anders's death...and its repercussions. Sometimes, Leo thought, he wondered if they'd ever be free of Anders's repercussions, the messes he made, the people he disappointed.

And Phoebe and her son were just another problem Leo had to solve. Leo took another long swallow of brandy and closed his eyes. He knew what was required of him; the king had made it clear. *Bring the son, pay off the girl.* So simple. So cold-hearted. So treacherous.

Already he doubted the success of such a plan. Phoebe showed a fierce and unwavering loyalty to her child, and no doubt an offer of cold cash would enrage her, as it had before, and entrench her even more deeply in her disgust of Amarnes and its royal family. A subtler tactic was needed, a more sophisticated deceit.

He needed to keep her pliable, sweet, until he could decide just what he would do with her. What he *wanted* to do with her... Leo felt a tightening in his gut as he thought of how she responded to his lightest touch... She was so transparent in her desire. And yet he felt it as well, deep inside, a need...

He pushed the thought—as well as the feeling—away. He couldn't afford to desire Phoebe. She was a problem to be solved, an inconvenience to be dealt with, just as she'd surmised all those years ago. Even now he remembered every word of the conversation, could feel the smooth silk of her skin against his questing hand...

No. He clamped down on the thought, straightening his shoulders, and tossed back the last of his brandy. As the first stars began to glimmer in the sky, he considered his next move.

CHAPTER FOUR

PHOEBE followed Sven up the thickly carpeted stairs, the long velvet curtains drawn against the night. Everything was silent and still, hushed and muted, so she could hear the relentless drumming of her own heart, loud in her ears.

Sven came to the end of an upstairs corridor and opened the door.

'Mommy!' Christian sprang up from where he'd been sitting with a scattered pile of Lego.

'Having fun?' Phoebe asked lightly, even as her arms ached to clasp her son to her in a tight hug and never let him go. Dash out of the consulate and run from the ever-grasping claws of the royal family, with their power and their ruthless arrogance.

'Yes…' Christian admitted a bit grudgingly. Looking around the room, Phoebe could see that was indeed the case. The sumptuous carpet was scattered with Lego and action heroes, and a pile of Christian's favorite DVDs rested by the large-screen plasma TV.

'Can we go?' Christian asked, and Phoebe saw him chew nervously on his lip. 'I'm hungry.'

'You can have dinner here,' Phoebe suggested. 'I'm sure they'll let you order whatever you like. You can have that pizza you wanted.'

'Of course,' Nora murmured.

'But I want to go now…'

So do I, Phoebe thought grimly, but she simply rested a hand lightly on Christian's head, resisting yet again the urge to grab him and run. 'Soon, I promise. Why don't you watch a DVD?' She gestured towards the huge television. 'You've been asking for one of those for ages.'

'I don't want to watch a DVD,' Christian said at his most obstinate, and Phoebe sighed, crouching down so she was at eye-level. 'Christian, I'm sorry, but we have to stay a bit longer. I told you I had some business to take care of, and it will be finished—soon. I need to talk to—to Prince Leopold for a few more minutes—'

'Prince?' Christian repeated, his voice sharpening with curiosity and then, worse, realisation. 'Like the prince on TV? The one who died?'

Phoebe silently cursed her son's mental agility. 'Ye-es,' she agreed reluctantly, adding a caveat, 'sort of.'

'You know a prince,' Christian said, sounding impressed, and then he actually puffed out his chest. 'And so do I.'

'A prince with a big-screen TV,' Phoebe reminded him, desperate for a diversion. 'I'll just be a few more minutes, OK?'

'OK.' Christian nodded slowly, won over by the promise of pizza and a DVD.

Phoebe straightened, smiling in relief, even as she steeled herself for another round with Leo. Yet at that moment all she could remember was that dark look of compassion in his eyes, and the way his fingers had burned through her coat.

Sven took her back downstairs, but instead of returning to the large reception room at the front of the consulate he led her to a smaller, more private room at the back.

He opened a door and ushered her inside, retreating and closing the door softly behind him before Phoebe even had a chance to register where she was.

'What is this?' she demanded, and Leo turned to her and smiled.

'Dinner, of course.'

But it wasn't just dinner, Phoebe acknowledged with a fluttering of panic she knew she shouldn't feel. It looked—and felt—like some kind of seduction.

The room was dimly lit by a few small table lamps, and a table for two had been laid by the marble fireplace, set with a creamy damask cloth, delicate porcelain and the finest crystal, glinting in the light. The flames of the fire cast leaping shadows over the room, and half of Leo's face was in shadow, so she could only see the faint curling of his mouth in what she supposed was a smile.

He looked far too confident, Phoebe thought as the panic rose, far too powerful, too predatory. Too sensual. For there could be no denying that Leo Christensen was a completely sensual being.

He'd taken off his tie and undone the top two buttons of his shirt so that Phoebe's gaze was instinctively drawn—as it had been six years ago—to the strong column of his throat. She jerked her gaze upwards, felt herself flush as she saw how Leo had been watching her. Knowing.

'I'm not hungry,' Phoebe said, taking a step towards the door.

'Aren't you?' Leo murmured, and Phoebe's flush intensified as though her whole body was burning. Burning not just with awareness, but with shame, for something about Leo invoked a helpless response in her that she hated.

Desire.

She felt it stretch and spiral between them, sleepy, seductive and far too powerful. No, Phoebe corrected fiercely, not desire. Fascination. It was like a child's fascination with fire, fingers aching to touch the flickering flame, so forbidden and dangerous. It didn't *mean* anything. It wouldn't, of course it wouldn't. She didn't even *like* Leo. As long as she remembered that and kept herself well away from the flames, she'd be all right. Safe.

Except now the source of heat and danger was walking right towards her with that long, easy stride, smiling with sleepy sensuality as he held out a glass of wine he'd just poured while she'd been standing here, her mouth hanging open and her eyes as wide as a child's, or worse, a lovesick girl's.

'Here.' He handed her the glass of wine, which Phoebe accepted before she could think better of it, her nerveless fingers curling around the fragile stem.

'You've gone to rather a lot of effort,' she finally said. Leo merely raised his eyebrows.

'I must admit I did little more than bark a few orders, but I thought we'd both be more comfortable having eaten something.'

'Did you?' Phoebe mumbled, taking a sip of wine, wishing she didn't feel this helpless fascination. Already she couldn't keep her eyes from wandering up and down the length of him, the long legs, trim hips and broad shoulders, finally resting on those full, sculpted lips, wondering how—

Stop. This was ridiculous. *Dangerous.*

'Yes, I did,' Leo replied, amusement gleaming in those golden, hooded eyes, eyes like an eagle's, the eagles that were stamped on every piece of priceless porcelain on the table, reminding her just who she was dealing with, *what*—

Phoebe put her glass down with an unsteady clatter. 'I appreciate your effort,' she said, forcing herself to meet Leo's gaze directly, 'but I'd really like to finish things here and go—'

'Home. Yes, I know. However, I'm afraid it's not going to be that simple or quick. And I, for one, am starving, having travelled across the Atlantic this afternoon with very little to eat.' He went to the table and began to remove the covers from several silver chafing dishes.

Leo began serving them both food, fragrant offerings that made Phoebe's stomach clench and rumble despite her protestations that she wasn't hungry. 'Come, sit down,' he said mildly. 'There's no reason to refuse to eat, is there?'

'I'm not—'

'Hungry? Yes, you are. I can hear your stomach rumbling from here. And if you're worried about Christian, I had Nora order pizza. He doesn't have any food allergies, I trust.' He spoke with such confidence Phoebe knew he'd already checked. Yet despite his knowing arrogance, she was touched that he had thought to consider Christian's needs. It was a small detail, irrelevant really, yet it still, strangely, meant something.

'Thank you,' she murmured, still somewhat grudgingly. 'Christian loves pizza.'

'Come.' He beckoned her, holding aloft a dish that was steaming and fragrant. 'You know you want to.'

Phoebe almost resisted simply for the principle of it. She didn't want to be seduced by Leo, not even by the food he offered. He was toying with her, she knew, teasing her because he knew he affected her, knew that there was something basic and primal that she responded to, helplessly, hopelessly.

She'd felt it back then, a little spark leaping to life deep inside her, and now she felt that spark flame to life once more, licking at her insides, threatening to burgeon into a full-grown inferno of need.

'Fine.' Phoebe moved over to the table and sat down, accepting the plate of boeuf Bourguignonne in its rich red wine sauce that Leo handed her. It smelled and looked delicious. 'And now you can tell me what this is all about.'

'Of course.' Leo took a sip of wine, watching her over the rim of his glass. 'Tell me, when was the last time you saw Anders?'

'That's hardly relevant,' Phoebe snapped. She shifted in her seat, uneasy at this line of questioning and where it might lead.

'I'm curious.'

'Too bad.' She took a bite of beef, barely registering the rich gravy or succulent meat. Her heart was thudding with heavy, hectic beats and her hands felt clammy. And all because of Leo. Why did she let him affect her this much?

'Did Anders ever meet his son?'

Phoebe pressed her lips together. 'Let's just say,' she said tightly, 'that he wasn't interested.'

'I see.' Leo gazed at her with a shrewd compassion Phoebe didn't like. She didn't want to be pitied or even understood. She just wanted to be left alone. 'All right, Phoebe,' Leo said. 'It's really rather simple. King Nicholas regrets his separation from Anders. He was furious six years ago, as you probably know—he'd already arranged Anders's marriage with a minor European royal when he announced his relationship with you. It would have been a good match.'

Phoebe's fingers clenched around the heavy sterling-silver fork. 'Maybe so, but Anders obviously thought differently.'

'Perhaps,' Leo replied, and Phoebe felt it as an insult, even though in essence it was true. Anders *had* felt differently...for about a month.

'I already know the king regrets his separation,' Phoebe said, and heard the impatience fraying her tone. 'You've made that abundantly clear. I just don't see what it has to do with me—'

'Nothing to do with *you*,' Leo replied blandly, 'but everything to do with Christian.' He smiled, that sensual mouth curving, curling, making Phoebe want to shiver. 'The king,' he told her, 'wishes to see his grandchild.'

Phoebe said nothing. Again, she found she wasn't surprised. Horrified, but not surprised. Wasn't this what she'd been waiting for, secretly, silently dreading? A claim on her child, no matter how small. A claim that could become stronger than her own. She opened her mouth, groping for words, for a cutting rebuttal, yet nothing came. Her mind was spinning in horrible circles, looking for an escape, some way out of this mess—

'In Amarnes,' Leo clarified in a terribly implacable tone. He paused. 'You're welcome to accompany him, of course.'

Outrage finally gave her voice. 'Of course I'll accompany him! That is, *if* he was going anywhere—which he's not.'

Leo gazed at her, rotating the stem of his wine glass between long, lean fingers. 'Phoebe,' he said finally, his voice surprisingly, strangely gentle, 'do you really think you can make such a statement?'

'I just did—'

'And back it up?' Leo cut her off, his voice still soft yet with a chilling knowledge that made Phoebe blink. And blink again.

'He's my child. I don't need to back anything up,' she finally said, but even to her own ears her voice sounded uncertain. Afraid.

'And my uncle is the king of a small but wealthy and well-connected country,' Leo told her. 'What he wishes, he gets. And frankly there isn't a court in the world that would rule in your favour. My uncle would make sure of it.'

'A court?' Phoebe repeated blankly, and a second later the single word caused a host of unpleasant connotations and images to tumble through her mind: trials and lawsuits, custody battles—all things she couldn't afford, not emotionally or financially. 'Your uncle would take me to court?'

Leo shrugged. 'If you refuse him this small request—'

'And how is this request small?' Phoebe demanded. She rose from the table, spinning away, her fists pressed to her eyes as if she could shut out Leo's voice, the reality he was forcing upon her.

From behind her she heard Leo rise from the table and come to stand behind her; she could feel the heat emanating from him, and for one crazy moment she wanted to lean back against him, feel the strength and hardness of his chest, find some kind of comfort there.

With *Leo*? her mind mocked. She really was falling apart if she thought there was any comfort to be had from him.

'I'm sorry,' he said in a tone that managed to be both compassionate and final, 'but this is how it is, and you cannot change it.' He paused. 'Prepare for a holiday in Amarnes. You might even enjoy it.'

Phoebe whirled around. 'For six years your family has completely ignored me. And now suddenly they want something from me? And think they can have it?'

Leo didn't even blink. 'Essentially, yes.' His voice was flat, but she thought she saw a flicker of compassion in his eyes, and in desperation she appealed to that faint, frail hope.

'Leo, please. It doesn't make sense to drag Christian from the home he loves, the life he knows, and for what? To appease an old man's sense of regret? It's not fair to me or to Christian.'

Leo hesitated, and for a moment—a second—Phoebe thought she had a chance. Prayed that he understood, that he'd relent—then his face closed, like a fan snapping shut, and despair fell over Phoebe like a dank fog.

'I'm sorry,' he said, his voice flat, expressionless. 'There is nothing I can do.' He gave a little shrug, dismissing her pain and distress in so tiny, so indifferent a gesture. 'It is only for a fortnight.'

Two weeks. Two weeks in Amarnes, facing the royal family, reliving that unwanted episode of her life. And would it end then? Phoebe wondered dully. Would King Nicholas be satisfied? Or would he just go on asking for—demanding—more, and more, and even more, until Phoebe and Christian's lives were siphoned away in sacrifice to an old man's selfish whims, drop by tiny drop, week by painful week.

She turned to Leo. 'And it will end there? We'll go home, and the king will never want to see us again?' She let out a sharp, incredulous laugh. 'You honestly expect me to believe that? That he won't want—demand—more?'

Leo's face was utterly impassive. 'Perhaps he will be satisfied,' he said. 'This might be no more than a passing fancy.'

'And that should make me feel better, I suppose,' Phoebe tossed back. 'I'm sure Christian will be happy to have served his purpose and then be thrown away like rubbish!'

Annoyance flashed across Leo's face like a streak of lightning. 'You are being melodramatic. There is no reason why a two-week trip to a beautiful country should be nothing but a lovely holiday for both you and your son. You look exhausted,' he continued bluntly, 'and I'm sure you could use some relaxation.'

'I'm hardly going to relax—'

'You might try,' Leo cut her off. 'It would certainly make the trip more pleasant for you.' His voice was sharp with impatience, and Phoebe knew he was done with her objections. Her fate, and her child's, had been decided. And there wasn't a single thing she could do about it.

She saw that now, starkly, understanding once again the kind of people—the kind of power—she was dealing with. She couldn't face a royal family in the courts. She couldn't face the tabloids and the paparazzi that would swarm over her little family like greedy vultures when they caught wind of this story.

'Come, why don't you eat?' Leo said mildly, sitting down again. Phoebe shook her head.

'Now I've really lost my appetite.'

'Suit yourself. But just because you don't like the state of affairs doesn't mean you can't enjoy yourself in the meantime.'

Phoebe glanced around the sumptuous room flickering with firelight, their decadent meal spread on the table. She thought of what she'd seen of Leo in the papers, years before, and wondered how many meals like this he'd enjoyed with the models and starlets he liked to have on his arm…and no doubt in his bed. A resentment she didn't quite understand spiked her voice as she said, 'Like you do, I suppose.'

There was a second's hesitation before Leo shrugged

and poured them both more wine, even though Phoebe's glass was still mostly full. 'Of course.'

Phoebe took a breath, opened her mouth and prepared for a fight. Yet suddenly, looking at the magnificently laid table and the remains of her delicious meal, she felt all the fight—all the anger and outrage and self-righteous fury— trickle out of her. Leo was right, even if she didn't want him to be. She had to accept this. The problems her refusal could cause were too dire to consider.

Two weeks in Amarnes, and then they could return home, to the life she'd built for them both here in New York. Two weeks in Amarnes, and Christian could get to know his father's side of the family. Perhaps she could even see the positive side of things, make it an adventure…

And in the meantime, she would eat and enjoy this meal. Resolutely she returned to the table and raised her wine glass to Leo in an ironic toast, earning her a faint smile. 'Very well,' she said stiffly. 'Cheers.'

'Cheers,' Leo murmured, and they both drank in silence. Phoebe fought the temptation to drain her glass.

'So,' she said when they'd both finished drinking and she'd picked up her fork, toying with a bit of beef. 'What's happened in Amarnes these last six years?'

'More of the same, really,' Leo replied in a deliberate drawl. 'Nothing much happens in these tiny little countries, you know, although we like to think it does.'

Phoebe choked back a surprised laugh. 'I suppose Anders's abdication was the news of the century, then.'

'Just about.'

'And it made you king.'

'Heir,' Leo corrected, his tone light although his expression had hardened. 'King Nicholas is still alive, as far as I know.'

Phoebe took another sip of wine. 'The Playboy Prince will become the Playboy King one day,' she quipped a bit sardonically, and Leo's mouth tightened, his eyes darkening to a deep umber. She wondered if she'd actually offended him. 'Your reputation is well-known, you know. At least it was when I—'

'Yes, I'm aware,' he said in a bored voice. 'Although in that regard, I suppose some things have changed in Amarnes.'

Phoebe regarded him curiously. Was he actually trying to say *he'd* changed? Yet he seemed so much the same— even as that thought took hold of her, another realisation swept through her. He *had* changed. Gone were the rumpled curls, as if he'd just risen from bed—from being with a lover. His hair was cut short, and more grey streaked his temples. And even though he'd treated her with the same lazy arrogance as he had six years ago, Phoebe sensed something new—something harder—in him now, a resolute sense of purpose that had been lacking before— or was she simply being fanciful? Imagining things, rewriting history, the man she'd known?

Except, Phoebe thought, she'd never really known Leo. She'd met him for ten minutes and read about him in the tabloids. That was all, and it occurred to her how very little it was. Now, suddenly—stupidly, perhaps—she found herself wondering just what kind of man he was. What kind of man he'd been, and then, more intriguingly, how he might have changed.

'So what have you been doing, then?' she finally asked. She took a bit of beef and chewed slowly, watching him. Swallowing, she continued. 'How have you been keeping yourself?'

Leo shrugged. 'A bit of this, a bit of that.'

'That's hardly an answer.'

'I'm sure a more specific answer would bore you. Do you really want to know the monotonous details of royal duty?'

'You're not a playboy any more?' Phoebe pressed.

Leo smiled, the sleepy, sensual smile Phoebe remembered, and as awareness coiled in her belly and raced through her veins she knew one thing that hadn't changed: her response to him.

'You know what they say. You can take the man out of the country, but you can't—'

'You mean,' Phoebe cut him off, 'you haven't changed?'

Leo shrugged. 'Judge for yourself. But...' he leaned forward, his eyes glinting into hers '...enough about the boring, sordid details of my own life. I want to know about you.'

Phoebe raised her brows, a strange, surprising smile lurking inside her, quirking her mouth. 'Can something be sordid *and* boring?'

'Most definitely.' He dismissed the topic with a shrug of one powerful shoulder. 'Now, I know a bit about how you've been keeping yourself—'

'How?'

Leo smiled. 'Phoebe, I always do my research.'

'You had me investigated?' she demanded sharply.

'Of course. That's how Christian's existence was discovered.'

'Why—why would you do that?' Phoebe asked in a whisper, thinking, *if only he hadn't...*

'I'm afraid when Anders died, he left a few skeletons in the cupboard that had to be dealt with. You were one of them.'

'And now you're dealing with me,' Phoebe filled in. 'Once again I'm an inconvenience.'

'But an interesting one,' Leo told her with a faint smile. 'I learned, for instance, that you have your own business, designing jewellery.'

Phoebe nodded, a sense of pride burgeoning within her when she thought of what she'd accomplished. 'Yes, I do. I have a small boutique on St Mark's Place and a mail-order service as well.'

'You've made a life for yourself,' Leo observed, and Phoebe's eyes flashed.

'Despite my supposedly squalid apartment?'

His answering smile took the sting out of her remark. 'I suppose your apartment could be seen as…adequate,' he said with a heavy sigh that made a reluctant smile tug at Phoebe's mouth. She could hardly believe she was sitting here, talking and laughing with Leo Christensen… almost as if they were friends.

Had he simply lulled her into a false sense of security, comfort? Or was this real?

She realised with a surprising pang of longing that she wanted it to be. Despite the fullness of her life, her business, her friends and family, she'd been without a man. A companion. With a son to raise and a growing business to manage there hadn't been time, or, Phoebe acknowledged, much inclination. The wreck of her one-month marriage kept her wary and distant, although she'd had a few relationships—well, dates at least—over the years.

Leo leaned forward, his fingers reaching out to touch Phoebe's throat, his fingers lightly caressing its hollow. 'Is this one of your pieces?'

Phoebe swallowed, far too affected by Leo's casual caress. His fingers were still brushing her skin as he touched the necklace, an uncut sliver of fiery agate encased in twisted gold wire.

'Yes...' Her voice came out in a shuddery hiss of breath. Leo looked up, and Phoebe was transfixed by his gaze, his eyes the same colour as the stone he caressed.

'It's beautiful. Unusual. I can see why you've been successful.'

'Thank you.' He was still touching her, and Phoebe knew she should withdraw, should demand he drop his hand. Yet she couldn't. She was enjoying it too much, savouring the feel of his fingers against his skin, revelling in the desire that uncoiled and wound its way through her.

Why was she so helpless when it came to this man? And did it even matter why? It simply *was*.

Leo's eyes met and clashed with hers, and after another heightened second he slowly—almost reluctantly—withdrew his hand. 'How did you get started in jewellery?' he asked. He leaned back in his chair, leaving Phoebe feeling stupidly, ridiculously, *overwhelmingly* bereft. She looked away, afraid Leo would see the disappointment in her eyes.

'My mother is a potter, and so art was always part of my upbringing. We'd go to Long Island for summer every year, and I loved collecting stones on the beach. Pretty ones, different ones. I'd twist string around them to make necklaces and bracelets and things.' She shrugged, suddenly self-conscious. 'And that's where my jewellery comes from, really. Childish crafts, but grown-up.'

'Very grown-up,' Leo murmured. 'I can't imagine it's cheap to rent retail space in Manhattan.'

'No, indeed,' Phoebe agreed. 'And apartments aren't cheap, either.'

'Touché.' Leo grinned, his eyes lightening to amber, his teeth strong and white. He raised his glass in a mock-toast. 'You're not going to forgive that one remark, are you?'

'Not any time soon,' Phoebe retorted, trying to be flippant although she felt far from it. Leo's full-fledged grin had had a devastating effect on her; she'd never seen him smile properly before, without irony or contempt or derision. She looked away, taking a slug of wine, willing her heart rate to slow. She couldn't keep on like this, every sense on high alert, responsive to his every gesture. Craving more.

One of the consulate's staff slipped in quietly to clear the remains of their meal. The fire snapped and crackled, and Phoebe knew she should go. Even more importantly, she should *want* to go. Yet somehow she didn't. Somehow she wanted to stay in this warm, comfortable room, with the fire casting leaping shadows along the panelled walls, and the glow of Leo's smile starting a fire in her soul. In her body, too, for her throat still burned where he'd touched her all too briefly.

Stop it. Phoebe closed her eyes in private supplication. *Please.* Wanting Leo was such a bad idea. It would cloud her judgement, make her weak…

She had to think of what was best for Christian, not her own unsatisfied body. She had to keep them both safe.

Somewhere in the consulate a clock struck eight, low, sonorous chimes that reverberated through Phoebe and made her reluctantly stir. 'I should go.' Yet she didn't move. 'It's late, and we can continue this discussion another day—'

'I'm afraid not,' Leo said, and he sounded genuinely regretful. 'You see, the king is not very well at the moment and he wants to see Christian as soon as possible. We need to leave for Amarnes tomorrow.' Phoebe's mouth dropped open in soundless shock. *Tomorrow…?* 'The arrangements have been made,' Leo continued, 'and I will fetch you and Christian at eight o'clock tomorrow morning.'

Her earlier stirrings of desire gave way to sheer outrage. 'That's impossible! I can't arrange travel details so quickly. Christian is in school and I'm not even sure his passport is current—'

Leo shrugged. 'Ring the school, and the passport is irrelevant. We will be travelling on a private jet, and—' his smile glimmered briefly '—I think Customs will let him through, as a royal.'

As a royal. Phoebe wasn't ready to process that statement or its frightening implications. She shook her head. 'And what about my work?'

Leo's expression didn't even flicker. 'Since you manage your own business, I'm quite certain you can arrange a leave of absence.'

'I have orders to fill—'

'And they can't wait for two weeks?' Leo raised his eyebrows. 'Surely you have an assistant of some kind who can do what is necessary. If not, hire one and the Amarnesian government shall pay for it.'

'Hire one by tomorrow morning?' Phoebe demanded, and Leo simply shrugged again.

'I do have an assistant,' she admitted grudgingly, 'but she's part-time and I can hardly ask—'

'Yes,' Leo replied, his tone managing to be both friendly and implacable, 'you can.'

Phoebe bit back yet another angry retort. She knew there was no point in arguing. Leo would meet each objection with that irritating indifference before reminding her once again of the royal family's power and reach. She was beaten…for the moment.

'Fine,' she finally said, her teeth gritted, 'but at the end of two weeks I'm returning home with Christian and I plan to never see any of you ever again.' The words sounded petulant, she knew, and also a bit desperate. Could she guarantee such a thing?

Leo regarded her for a moment, his head tilted to one side, those amber eyes softened in what, once more, unsettlingly, looked like compassion. 'Yes,' he said, his voice carefully expressionless, 'of course you are.'

The fire had died to a few embers in the grate, the moon a lonely silver sickle high above in the sky as Leo poured himself another brandy. Phoebe had left with Christian hours ago, and now he pictured her putting her little boy to bed in her apartment, sitting alone on the sofa, her knees drawn up to her chest as she contemplated her changed and uncertain future.

And she had no idea just how changed and uncertain it was. Leo smiled grimly. King Nicholas had not wanted Phoebe to come to Amarnes at all; he simply wanted the boy. Yet Leo knew that was an impossible task, and one he had no wish to perform. He wouldn't—couldn't—separate the boy from his mother, not when she was so obviously attached to him. He knew what that felt like, remembered his mother's pale, stricken face as she left on the royal jet for her home country of Italy, while Leo, six years old and stoic, stood silently at the nursery window, trying not to cry.

From that moment his life had been consecrated to the crown, to serve it and yet never wear it. For the last six years he'd been considered the heir apparent, much to Nicholas's fury. Leo knew Nicholas would rather have the monarchy crumble to nothing than have him as his successor, yet he had had no choice. And for the last six years Leo had been doing his damnedest to prove to Nicholas and to the people of Amarnes—to the whole world—that he was worthy of the crown.

'*Have you changed?*'

Phoebe didn't believe he had; she still saw him as a reckless playboy, cut from the same cloth as Anders. And perhaps he was. The old, familiar guilt, as corrosive as acid, roiled in his gut.

'*You don't deserve it…you don't deserve to be king.*'

Yet he would be, deserving or not. He was his uncle's only heir now, and nothing could change that. Anders's abdication was absolute. So Leo would continue to serve his country and his sovereign, and do what was required of him…no matter what it meant for Phoebe.

He drained the last of his brandy and stood up, preparing for bed. He couldn't afford to think about Phoebe, her feelings…or the way she'd felt when he touched her. For a moment he savoured the memory of the silkiness of her skin, how her grey eyes had darkened to slate, her lush body almost quivering with desire…

And he'd felt it too, a current running through him, hot and electric, needing an outlet. He still felt it now; his body was restless and unsated, yet Leo knew he would have to ignore it. Seducing Phoebe was not part of his plan. Couldn't be.

Yet what was his plan? Leo mused. He would bring them both to Amarnes, even though Nicholas would be furious. Perhaps the old man would grow bored and let them go, as Phoebe so obviously hoped, yet Leo doubted it. And what would Phoebe do then? Leo rubbed his face tiredly. He had no answers, not yet, but at least he'd done his duty. He always did his duty. He was bringing the boy back, and Phoebe—for the moment at least—was proving to be biddable. The rest, he decided, would have to wait.

CHAPTER FIVE

PALE sunshine slanted through the gauzy curtains of
Phoebe's bedroom as she slowly swung her legs over the
side of her bed and rested her head in her hands. It had only
taken a second of consciousness for the comforting veil
of sleep to be ripped away, replaced by the clamorous
memories of last night.

Leo. Leo was here in New York, and would be coming
to fetch them to take them to Amarnes in—she looked at the
clock and felt a lurch of panic. In less than two hours.
Quickly Phoebe rose from the bed, showered and dressed
before Christian woke up and demanded his breakfast. She
peeked in on Christian, and saw him sprawled across his
sheets.

When she'd taken him home from the consulate he'd
been bubbling over, fear so easily replaced by excitement.
Phoebe had told him they were going to Amarnes for two
weeks, preparing herself for questions, demands, even
tears. But Christian's eyes had simply widened and he'd
breathed one word: '*Cool*.' Five-year-olds, even ones as
precocious as her son, were easily appeased.

She'd also had to break the news to her mother, Amelia,
in Brooklyn. She'd called her mother after Christian was

asleep, her heart aching slightly at the sound of her cheerful hello.

'What's up?'

'A lot, actually,' Phoebe had said, trying for a laugh, but her mother, as always, heard the concern and worry underneath.

'Phoebe, what's wrong?'

Phoebe knuckled her forehead and closed her eyes, fighting a sudden, overwhelming wave of weariness. 'Two government agents from Amarnes showed up at my door a few hours ago.'

'What?' Her mother's breath came out in a hiss of surprise. She knew everything about Phoebe's hasty marriage to Anders; she'd been waiting at the airport with a hug and a smile when Phoebe arrived, weary and heart-sore, with a three-month-old Christian in her arms. 'Why?'

Phoebe pressed her lips together before she said shortly, 'Christian.'

Her mother was silent. 'They don't…'

'No,' Phoebe said quickly. 'They don't. And they won't know if I can help it.'

'Oh, Phoebe.' Phoebe nearly buckled under her mother's compassion. She was just about holding it together, making herself see this as the little adventure she'd promised Christian it was, but hearing the sorrow and worry in her mother's tone made Phoebe want to cry and confess all her fears.

What if they want him? What if they keep him? What if there are custody battles and lawsuits and horrible things I can't control? I'm so afraid.

She didn't give voice to any of these questions, merely continued in a rather flat voice, 'We're leaving tomorrow for Amarnes.'

'No—'

'For two weeks,' Phoebe clarified. 'Apparently the king wants to see his grandson. And then we'll come home.'

'Phoebe, don't give in to them. Once you're in Amarnes you'll have very few resources, very little power—'

'I have no choice, Mom,' Phoebe said. 'They're royal. They have millions. Billions, probably, and if it came to a court case—'

'Will it?' her mother asked quickly and Phoebe closed her eyes once more.

'I hope not. I pray not. But…I don't know.' Her hand felt slippery around the receiver. 'If I go willingly now, it might…help me later.'

'Or not,' Amelia said darkly and Phoebe blew out an exasperated sigh.

'Then what should I do?'

'I have a friend, a human-rights lawyer…' Phoebe could hear her mother scrabbling for one of the many business cards she kept stuck on her fridge with colourful magnets.

'Oh, Mom, I can't afford a lawyer. Not for the kind of court case we're talking about, and I don't want to drag Christian through that anyway.' Besides, she added silently, she doubted one of her mother's hippie friends, leftovers from the flower-power days of the sixties, would give her much credibility in court. 'Anyway,' she continued, keeping her voice firm, 'I've been thinking that Nicholas should see Christian anyway. I always felt the way they cut Anders out of their lives was so unfair, and I'd be a hypocrite to do the same thing with Christian.'

'Phoebe, these people don't deserve your sympathy—'

'Perhaps not,' Phoebe agreed, 'but that doesn't mean I'm going to be like them.' Strong words, she knew. She only wished she felt as strong and certain inside.

After speaking to her mother, she'd called her assistant, Josie, who had been more than happy to take over the boutique for two weeks.

It was, Phoebe thought, all too easy to arrange, almost as if it were meant to be. And perhaps it was. If she simply clung to the belief that this was for merely two weeks, she could be generous. She could allow the king access to her son, she could forgive them all for being so cold-hearted and bloody-minded, she could accept that Leo was simply doing what he had to do...

Leo. And, Phoebe asked herself with uncomfortable shrewdness, did any of this have to do with Leo, with the wellspring of desire he'd plumbed in her, with the memory of his brief touch still burning up her senses? Was all this magnanimity simply because she wanted a chance to see Leo again?

He's a playboy, a rake, a reprobate, Phoebe lectured herself, but the words bounced off her heart meaninglessly. She didn't know *what* Leo was any more. And this trip to Amarnes gave her a chance to find out.

Now, as morning broke, the Washington Square Arch bathed in the pink light of dawn, Phoebe steeled herself for the day ahead. She'd packed quickly last night, throwing in most of their clothes as well as a few of Christian's books and toys. She dressed simply in grey wool trousers and a pale pink sweater and tried to ignore the flutter of nerves—or was it actually excitement?—in her stomach.

The next hour passed in a flurry as Christian awoke and Phoebe rushed to get breakfast and pack last-minute things. Harassed and her hair half-brushed, Phoebe watched in dismay as a limousine with tinted windows pulled up to the apartment building, idling at the kerb. Her heart leapt into her throat as she watched Leo, dressed superbly in a dark suit, a wool trenchcoat over one arm, exit the car and press the bell.

Leo's dark gaze swept over the apartment building with its crumbling steps and soot-stained walls. It was charming, he supposed, in a slightly run-down way. His lips twitched as he imagined teasing Phoebe about it, before he clamped down on that thought. He couldn't afford it, couldn't allow Phoebe to matter at all. It would only hurt them both in the end.

Leo pressed the bell again, impatience biting at him. He knew this had to be difficult for Phoebe, knew it was the last thing she wanted, and who could blame her? The royal family had spat her out six years ago and now they wanted to chew her back up. Hardly an enticing proposition, yet one she would have to accept, just as he had.

He pictured her then, not as he remembered her six years ago with her still childishly rounded face and college student's clothes of torn jeans and a T-shirt, but the woman she'd become. The woman he'd seen yesterday, whose hair was still curly and dark, whose slight figure still possessed improbably lush curves. He thought of how her wide grey eyes sparked defiance—and an irrepressible desire—when she looked at him.

It infuriated her perhaps, that desire, but it was there. It had been there last night; he'd seen it, *felt* it humming in the air between them when she'd entered the room and had seen the candlelit room with a meal laid out like a planned seduction.

Of course, he couldn't seduce her, as much as his body begged for that release. Sex was a complication he couldn't afford. Last night had simply been a way to gain her confidence, her trust, even her friendship.

He needed Phoebe pliant and willing, ready to do the royal family's bidding…whatever it might be.

Phoebe called for Christian, who had been racing around the apartment like a wild thing, and reached for her suitcase. She didn't want Leo in her apartment, filling up the small space with his formidable presence, yet she realised it was unavoidable as she heard his tread on the stairs, light yet purposeful. Mrs Simpson must have let him in, Phoebe thought. She never could resist a handsome face or a charming smile, and Leo had both.

And then he was there, knocking on the door, which Christian wrenched open before Phoebe could stop him—not that there would be any point, delaying the utterly inevitable.

'Hello.' Leo stood in the doorway, dressed in a dark suit, looking calm and unruffled and unusually solemn. He surveyed Christian, who stared at him in open curiosity. 'My name is Leo, and I suppose I'm your cousin.'

Christian's eyes widened. 'I have a cousin?'

Leo's gaze moved questioningly to Phoebe, who bit her lip. 'We hadn't quite got round to discussing that yet,' she said quietly and Leo inclined his head.

'Well, it's quite a nice surprise for you, isn't it, Christian?' He smiled easily. 'I like surprises. Do you?'

'Ye-es,' Christian agreed after a moment, and Leo reached for the rather large, green plastic dinosaur poking out of Christian's backpack.

'My goodness, I wouldn't want this fellow to catch me in a dark alley,' he said, inspecting the toy with considerable interest. 'He's got a lot of teeth, hasn't he?'

'And he makes a noise, too,' Christian said eagerly, pushing a button so the dinosaur let out a fearsome mechanical roar and clawed the air for a few seconds. Leo let out a little yelp, pretending to jump back in fright, thus earning a great belly laugh from Christian. 'It's just pretend,' he said with a child's scorn, and Leo returned it to his backpack.

'Thank goodness for that,' he said, his eyes meeting Phoebe's over Christian's head. Phoebe smiled in gratitude, amazed and thankful at how effortlessly Leo had diverted Christian from the thorny question of his relations. Yet Leo was charming, always had been; why not with children as well as women? That was why he was so dangerous.

'We should go,' she said a bit stiltedly, conscious of Leo's warm gaze on her, as well as the fact that she hadn't had time to blow-dry her hair. It framed her face in wild, dark curls, and she could see Leo eyeing them. Did she not look smart enough? He turned back to Christian.

'Yes, we should. The car, not to mention the royal jet, is waiting.'

'Royal jet?' Christian repeated, and his eyes bugged out. 'Really?'

'Yes, Amarnes is an island. We'll take my limousine to the airport, and fly from there.'

'Wow.' Christian looked completely thrilled now, and Phoebe managed a smile.

'Pretty cool, eh?' she said, keeping her voice light even as her heart hammered within her in a staccato beat that seemed to say *two weeks, two weeks, two weeks*. Only two weeks.

Leo stepped in front of her, taking the suitcase from her with an easy smile. 'Please. Allow me.'

'Thank you,' she murmured and with Christian by her side she followed Leo down the stairs.

They didn't speak as he loaded the cases in the back of the limo himself, or even when they arranged themselves on the plush leather seats, Christian's eyes wide as he took in the mini-bar and fresh flowers.

Leo slipped into the limo across from her, and she was achingly aware of his presence, his heat, his scent. Her fingers felt thick and clumsy as she fumbled with Christian's seat belt, wishing her senses were not so heightened when it came to Leo and yet craving it—him—anyway.

'Here.' Quietly, competently, Leo clicked Christian's buckle closed, his long brown fingers over hers. Touching hers. And in her emotionally heightened state, Phoebe felt a rush of something—what? Gratitude, or something more? No, something less, something so basic, this fascination with Leo, with his aura of excitement and danger.

Except right now he wasn't being dangerous. He was just being kind.

'Thank you,' she mumbled before sitting back and buckling her own seat belt.

'Not a problem.' Leo leaned back against his seat, stretching his legs in front of him. 'Now, Christian, would you like something to drink? I think there's orange juice in the fridge, as well as some cola if your mother allows it.'

'Christian doesn't...' Phoebe began, but her son was already leaning forward to inspect the contents of the mini-bar.

'All right, fine,' she finally said, striving for that light tone once more. 'This is a holiday after all.'

'Exactly.' Leo smiled, and Phoebe tried to ignore the

effect of that gesture on her insides, tried to think of something else—anything else—as the limo pulled away from the kerb and headed into town, towards the Holland Tunnel.

They rode in silence to a private airstrip on the outskirts of the city. A sleek silver jet waited there, with the recognisable emblem of the twin eagles emblazoned on its tail.

'Wow,' Christian breathed as they boarded the plane. Leather sofas and a mahogany coffee table adorned with yet more freshly cut flowers made Phoebe feel as if she were entering a living room rather than an airplane. Christian was looking at all the luxury with wide eyes, and Phoebe tried to suppress a spurt of anxiety. She'd been afraid the royal family would want more of Christian…but what if he wanted more of them? How could she compete with all of this?

'Just enjoy it,' Leo murmured, his lips nearly brushing her ear, his breath fanning her cheek. Uneasily Phoebe wondered if she'd spoken aloud. Or had Leo just read her mind?

She chose not to answer, busying herself with settling Christian. Soon enough they were all seated and the plane was gliding down the runway and then up into a grey November sky.

'I've never been on a plane before,' Christian said after a few minutes of rather tense silence. His cheeks were flushed and he was clutching his dinosaur to him. 'That I remember, anyway.'

Leo glanced at him, his features seeming to soften. 'Then this should be quite an adventure for you.'

'I guess so,' Christian mumbled, shooting Phoebe an uncertain look. Phoebe knew that underneath the excitement her son was confused, and she would have to talk to him soon. Explain…except how could she explain? She wasn't even sure what was going to happen, and the last thing she wanted to do was tell him about relatives who might ultimately reject him.

Two weeks, her mind reminded her, her heart still beating fast. *Two weeks, two weeks, two weeks*.

The next few hours passed in silence punctuated only by Christian's occasional question—did they have pizza in Amarnes, and what about milkshakes?—as well as the tinny roar of his dinosaur as he played.

Phoebe sat tensely across from him, watching as Leo took out a sheaf of papers and a gold-plated pen and set to work. What was he working on? she wondered. What kind of work did a playboy prince have to do? Except he wasn't a playboy prince any more, she reminded herself. He was the heir apparent.

'What are you doing?' she asked when Christian had fallen into a doze and the silence seemed to stretch on for ever, taut and unyielding. Leo glanced up.

'A pet project of mine,' he said with a little shrug. 'Facts and figures, very boring.'

'You're quick to dismiss many things as boring,' Phoebe replied, and with surprise she heard the teasing lilt in her voice. Was she actually flirting? Or just being friendly?

Leo shrugged again. 'It's a charity,' he said after a moment. 'I'm one of the trustees and I'm simply going over the endowment figures.'

'What kind of charity?' Phoebe asked, now genuinely curious.

'A relocation programme for political refugees. Amarnes was a neutral country during World War Two, and we took in many of those fleeing persecution. I like to see the tradition continue today.'

'Very admirable,' Phoebe said, yet her mind was spinning. This new version of Leo—a man who concerned himself with refugees—bore little resemblance to the pleasure-seeking playboy she'd encountered six years ago.

Had he really changed so much? Yet his smile was as sardonic as ever as he remarked in a drawl, 'It's easy to be admirable when you have the money and time.' He capped his pen and put his papers away. 'You should get some sleep. The jet lag can be brutal.' And, seeming to dismiss her, he settled back in his own seat and closed his eyes.

Although he kept his eyes closed, sleep remained elusive. Leo was aware of the uncomfortable prickling of his conscience as he'd spoken with Phoebe. He wanted to gain her trust, he needed her pliant, and the best way to do that was to show her how he'd changed. How he was on her side. It would be all too easy, and yet when the opportunities came Leo found he didn't want to take them. He didn't want to use Phoebe. He wanted to...*protect* her. What a ridiculous and inappropriate notion. The only reason he was bringing her to Amarnes at all was because he knew he couldn't pay her off in New York. Sooner or later he would find a way to keep her out of the picture—or at least removed from it.

Just like your own mother was.

His jaw clenched and he forced his conscience back into the shadowy corner of his mind, where it had remained for most of his playboy years. Back then he hadn't had a conscience because he hadn't cared; he was the unneeded spare, and so he'd do what he damn well liked.

Yet Anders's abdication had changed everything. Leo felt the familiar guilt eat at him and he pushed it resolutely away. For the last six years he'd lived the life of a monk, a *saint*, chaste and diligent, and had won the respect of his people. He'd put his country and crown first, always, and he would continue to do so. No matter what it cost him...or Phoebe.

They were more important than the tender feelings of a woman he couldn't afford to care about. He shouldn't even want to care, he told himself irritably. Phoebe was an inconvenience, that was all. All she could be.

Forcing himself to relax, to forget that woman sitting across from him with every anxiety and fear reflected in her wide grey eyes even as she kept her tone light and upbeat for the sake of her son, Leo finally—by sheer force of will—drifted into a doze.

Phoebe couldn't sleep. Christian was snoring, his cheek pillowed against the plastic back of his dinosaur, and even Leo seemed to have dozed off, yet Phoebe sat there, tense, anxious, too many emotions and questions and desires coursing through her. What would happen when they arrived in Amarnes? How would the king receive Christian...and her? What was she going to *do*?

Too many questions, and none of them had answers. Yet. Phoebe pushed them away, and her gaze fell on Leo's sleeping form. He'd shed his jacket and rolled up the sleeves of his crisp white shirt, exposing strong, tanned forearms now loosely crossed. Phoebe's gaze fell on those arms and stayed there, noticing the fine dark hairs, the sinewy muscles, the long, elegantly tapered fingers. She knew she should look away—she should want to look away—but she couldn't.

That dark tug of fascination was pulling at her insides, and while Leo slept she found her gaze roving over him almost hungrily, noting the cropped, dark hair, the chiselled cheekbones and sculpted lips, the ridiculously long eye-lashes. She let her gaze drop from his face to his shoulders—how did a plain white shirt emphasise the powerful muscles of his chest so wonderfully?—and lower still to his trim waist and hips and long legs, stretched out in front of him, his butter-soft leather loafers just inches from her own feet.

He was a beautiful man. A dark angel with the heart of a devil...or so he'd seemed all those years ago. But now...?

'What would have happened, do you suppose, if you'd met me first?'

The question he'd asked her six years ago slipped slyly into her mind, and the answer Phoebe had given back then—nothing—seemed to echo uselessly through her.

All right, so she was attracted to him. Phoebe straightened in her seat and forced herself to look away, out of the window. The plane had risen above the city fog and now there were only a few wisps of cottony cloud in an otherwise perfect blue sky.

Of course she was attracted to him; he positively oozed sexuality and charm. And, to be perfectly blunt, she'd been without male companionship of any kind for too long.

Yet it still shamed her to admit to something so basic, so impossible to ignore or deny. How could she be attracted to Leo, the man who had insulted her, belittled her, tried to buy her? Was she so enslaved to her own senses?

Again Phoebe felt that dark tug of longing, of need.

Apparently she was.

'You mean you haven't changed?'

'Judge for yourself.'

Was it possible that Leo had really changed, put his playboy days behind him? She thought of him bantering with Christian, the glimmer of humour in his amber eyes, and forced back another treacherous wave of desire and, worse, hope.

She couldn't afford to believe Leo had changed. As much as she wanted to, she couldn't afford to trust him. She was on her own here, and she'd better remember that.

'Look.' Leo reached over and touched her shoulder, causing Phoebe to jump as if he'd branded her with a hot poker. She must have fallen into a doze without realising it. 'Amarnes,' he told her, and, swallowing audibly, Phoebe refocused her gaze on the vista outside.

Amarnes. It nestled in a slate-blue North Sea, a tiny, perfect jewel. The eastern side of the island was carved into deep fjords; from the sky Phoebe could see the steep sides of the valleys they created, lush and green, their rocky peaks capped with snow. As the plane moved over the fjords, Phoebe saw a cluster of brightly painted fishermen's cottages near the shore, and then, on a plain on the northern end of the island, Amarnes's capital city, Njardvik.

For a moment Phoebe let herself remember the last time she'd come to Amarnes, standing on the deck of a ferry, the salt spray stinging her face, Anders at her side. Back then she hadn't known Anders was a prince, hadn't known anything. She'd met him ten days earlier, while backpacking through Norway, and she'd fallen for him right away. Anders had had a gift of making her feel as if she were permanently fixed at the centre of his universe. It was only later—when a single piece of paper declared them married—that she realized he made *everyone* feel that way.

On the ferry he'd pointed to Amarnes, just a smudge of dark green on the horizon, and said, 'That's my home.' He had leaned against the railing and with a self-conscious smile added, 'I should probably tell you, I'm a prince.'

Phoebe had laughed disbelievingly, until Anders explained that he wasn't joking; he was actually heir to a throne. Phoebe had stared.

'I don't want any of it,' he'd told her. 'You can't imagine the pressure, the expectations.' His brilliant blue eyes had met and held hers. 'I just want you, Phoebe.'

What a joke. An outright lie. Anders might have believed it at that moment, Phoebe thought fairly, but it was simply that. A moment. Yet six years on Phoebe couldn't summon the energy to feel bitter or angry. She'd been as reckless as Anders, plunging into a marriage with a man she barely knew, and now that he was dead she only felt a distant kind of sorrow and even pity for the man he'd been and the life he'd wasted.

The plane began its descent, and Christian stirred. Phoebe's gaze slid involuntarily to Leo, and she was unsettled to realise he'd been watching her, his lips curved in a knowing smile that she didn't like.

'Welcome home,' he said softly, just for her ears, and Phoebe bristled.

'Hardly.'

Leo just smiled.

The next few minutes were a blur as they exited the plane, the cold, clean air hitting Phoebe like a slap—she'd forgotten how fresh everything was here, so new and bright and clean. Even the colours seemed sharper, the deep green of the fir trees that flanked the winking blue sea, the grey, craggy mountains with their majestic white peaks. And the sleek black limousine that purred to a halt as Leo directed their luggage to be loaded in a van and ushered them into the car.

'The palace is only a few minutes away,' Leo said as the limousine pulled away from the airstrip, heading down a narrow road that snaked along the valley floor. Phoebe glanced at Christian; he was taking in everything with wide, amazed eyes. He must, Phoebe thought, feel as if he'd stepped into a TV show, or a fairy tale.

Within minutes the limousine emerged from the closed valley to the outskirts of Njardvik, the boulevard into the city lined with pastel-coloured townhouses, a leftover relic of the island's Dutch possession four hundred years earlier. Unwillingly Phoebe gazed around at the quaint plazas with their flowerpots and pavement cafés, now shuttered for the oncoming winter. There could be no denying that Njardvik was an unspoiled jewel of a city, and just the sight of its pretty streets and elegant homes made her remember the optimism and excitement that had buoyed her along this very route with Anders.

Was her hope that this would end after two weeks just as misplaced?

'Wow,' Christian breathed, and Phoebe turned to see the limousine enter the eagle-crested gates of the palace court-yard. The palace itself was several hundred years old, a rambling and impressive edifice of mellow gold stone. A rather grim-faced official in royal livery waited by the main entrance, guarded by two soldiers resplendent in their royal blue uniforms and polished helmets.

'Here we are,' Leo said lightly, and opened the door.

Numbly Phoebe followed him, Christian clutched in her arms. She heard Leo speak a few words of Danish to the official, who opened the doors to the palace and, with a sweep of his arm, bade them enter.

She'd only been to the palace once before, hustled like some criminal by royal agents, afraid, alone, to be con-fronted by Leo. It almost made Phoebe feel dizzy and sick to be back here. Once again she was afraid, alone, and she had no idea what was going to happen.

She pushed the feelings away, tried to summon back her courage. Her confidence. She was changed, no matter if Leo was or wasn't. She was stronger now, and she had to remind herself of that strength as she stood in the palace's huge foyer, feeling tiny and insignificant on about an acre of black and white checked marble.

'The king would like to see you,' Leo said. 'But first you will want to rest, freshen up. Johann will lead you to your rooms.' Another servant, also in royal livery, seemed to appear almost magically, and wordlessly Phoebe followed him from the cool marble foyer up the ornate curving staircase, Christian at her side.

Johann led them to a suite of rooms in the back of the palace. Phoebe took in the two king-sized bedrooms, joined by an elegant little parlour, and the wide terrace overlooking the palace gardens, now rimed in frost.

She dropped her handbag next to her suitcase on the floor, the carpet thick and sumptuous, and took a deep, steadying breath. Christian was already investigating the huge walk-in wardrobes, the big-screen plasma TV hidden behind mahogany doors, the king-sized bed with its fluffy feather mattress.

'This place is so cool,' he said, reaching for the TV's remote control and stabbing curiously at the buttons. 'How long are we staying?'

'Two weeks,' Phoebe replied tightly. She felt wound up, ready to snap, and they hadn't even seen the king yet. They hadn't seen anything, done anything, and already the tension was biting at her, fraying her calm, her strength. She went to the bathroom to splash water on her face, and grimaced at her pale, strained reflection.

Christian wandered in, the remote control still clutched

in one hand. 'If the prince is my cousin, what should I call him?' he asked, wrinkling his nose. 'And if he is a prince, does that make me one too?'

A light knock on the door kept Phoebe from answering those alarming questions. She opened the door to another blank-faced servant, who informed her in flawless English that King Nicholas awaited in the throne room.

'Already?' Phoebe asked, to which the servant simply gave a helpless little shrug. She hadn't changed or even brushed her hair, but if the king was going to be so rude as to demand her attendance before she'd even caught her breath, he could take her as she was.

She gestured to Christian and, ever ready for an adventure, he quickly trotted to her side. They followed the servant through a maze of corridors and down another, more private staircase until finally they were standing in front of a pair of ornate doors decorated in gold leaf.

Phoebe swallowed. This part of the palace she'd never seen.

'His Majesty, King Nicholas the First of Amarnes,' a servant intoned, and the doors were thrown open. Phoebe started forward, Christian at her side, only to have a burly, solemn-faced servant step straight in front of her, so she smacked into his chest.

'What—?' she cried in dazed confusion. A hand came down hard on her shoulder.

'Only the boy,' a voice, low and final, spoke in clipped English, and before Phoebe could frame a protest she was hustled away as Christian disappeared behind the heavy, ornate doors.

CHAPTER SIX

'*WHAT?*' Leo looked up from the mail he'd been rifling through, his brows drawn sharply together in a frown. His top aide, Piers Handsel, gave a nod of confirmation.

'I thought you'd like to know. The king summoned the boy ten minutes ago.'

'But they've just arrived,' Leo said, his voice no more than a growl. Had the king no tact, no sensibility? Running roughshod over Phoebe was not the way to gain her trust.

'Just the boy,' Piers clarified. 'Not…' he paused delicately '…the mother.'

Leo dropped the letter he'd been holding and glared at his aide. 'What do you mean?' he asked, his voice menacingly soft.

Piers shrugged in apology. 'The king has no wish to see her, apparently. He refused her entrance into the throne room.'

'She would have resisted—'

Piers coughed. 'I believe Lars escorted her to the blue salon.'

'Lars!' Leo repeated in disgust. Lars was little more than a thug, paid to do Nicholas's dirty work. And when Piers said *escorted*, Leo had no doubt he really meant *forced*. So, only minutes after arriving at the palace, Phoebe was being treated like an unwanted prisoner, and her son was alone with the king. A stranger.

Rage, white-hot and electric, coursed through Leo. For a moment a memory of his own mother's treatment blazed through him. Just like Phoebe, she'd been shunted from the palace and her son's life because she'd been surplus to requirements. He felt sick at what Phoebe had to endure. What he had allowed her to endure.

'I will speak to the king,' he said shortly and, tossing the rest of his mail aside, he strode from the room. Rage fuelled him as he navigated the palace's many corridors before arriving at the throne room. He paused at the doors, for if Christian was still with the king he had no desire to frighten the boy. All was silent from within. Leo threw open the doors and strode in.

Nicholas sat on the throne, a small, grey-haired man, diminished by age, wearing his usual three-piece suit, his thin, liver-spotted hands folded over his middle.

Leo didn't bother with the preliminaries; he was too angry. 'What were you thinking,' he demanded tersely, 'to separate Phoebe from her child practically the moment they arrived?'

Nicholas regarded his nephew shrewdly. 'Phoebe, is it? I told you not to bring her.'

'I had no choice,' Leo replied, his voice curt despite the anger that still coursed through him. He curled his hand into a fist at his side, resisting the urge to plough it straight into the king's sagging belly. 'She wouldn't be bought.'

'Everyone can be bought.'

Leo pressed his lips together. 'Phoebe is utterly dedicated to her son. I've seen it myself.' He paused. 'Before I went to New York, I didn't realise quite how much.' He'd gone to New York anticipating a flighty, careless woman… the kind of woman who had married a man she'd known for little more than a week, and separated from a month later. Yet Phoebe hadn't been that woman. She'd changed, he realised, changed and grown, and he felt a surprising flash of both pride and admiration at the thought.

Nicholas shrugged. 'No matter. I'm sure we can find a way to dispose of her.'

Dispose of her. Like rubbish, Leo thought, just as Phoebe had feared. Twenty-four hours ago such a statement would have caused barely a ripple of unease; Phoebe had just been an inconvenience to deal with. Yet now his uncle's callousness infuriated him. Enraged him, touching and hurting him in a deep place inside he couldn't bear to think about. 'Your sensitivity astonishes me,' he said in a clipped voice that belied the emotion coursing through him in an unrelenting river, 'but she has a legal right to her son—'

'As did your mother,' Nicholas replied with a glimmer of a smile. 'Yet she saw fit to step aside.'

Leo struggled to speak calmly; the mention of his mother caused that river of emotion flowing through him to become a torrent, an unstoppable tide. For a moment he was that boy again, standing at the window, struggling not to cry, yet wanting desperately to shout out, to beg her to come back or at least turn around. She never had.

Mio Dio, did he see himself in Christian? His mother in Phoebe? How could he have ever considered separating them for a moment?

Yet he hadn't, Leo realised. From the moment he'd entered the salon at the consulate and seen Phoebe standing there, so proud and afraid, so much the same as he remembered with her wide grey eyes, as clear as mirrors, and her dark, curly hair, irrepressible and wild…his plans to buy her off had disappeared. Evaporated, like so much meaningless mist. He would never separate a mother from her child…yet what could he do with her now? What life could she have in Amarnes? Or would the king tire of the boy as Phoebe hoped?

'What do you intend,' he asked now, trying to sound unconcerned, 'with the boy?'

Nicholas shrugged. 'I like him,' he said, his tone that of a child with a new toy. 'He has courage. He was obviously afraid when he entered the throne room, but he didn't succumb to tears. He threw back his shoulders and greeted me like a man.' Nicholas paused, and Leo turned around to see the king give him a sly, sideways smile. 'He will make a good king.'

For a moment all Leo could do was stare blankly at the king as his words echoed through him. '*He will make a good king…a good king…a good king…*' 'What,' he finally asked with soft menace, 'do you mean?'

Nicholas chuckled. 'You didn't realise, did you? Why do you think I sent for the boy?' Nicholas's mouth twisted cynically. 'To play happy families?'

Leo didn't trust himself to answer. Suddenly he realised how ridiculously sentimental, how glaringly *false* Nicholas's desire to see his grandson was. Of course he had an ulterior motive…but *king*?

'Anders abdicated,' Leo finally said in a low voice. 'You can't undo—'

'Can't I?' Nicholas looked positively gleeful, causing rage to course through Leo once more. Rage and regret and guilt, all wrapped together, consuming him, choking him— He'd been so blind. So blind to follow the king's bidding, to ignore his own memories, to bring Phoebe and

Christian here—to think he could be king. That he deserved to be.

'I've called a session of Parliament,' Nicholas said. He sat back on the throne, an ageing tyrant still determined to wield his power. To hurt.

'And just like that,' Leo demanded in a hiss, 'you're going to change the line of succession, make a child you don't even know your heir—?'

'The line of succession is intact,' Nicholas informed him coldly. 'You were the aberration.'

Of course he was. He always had been. The older son of the younger brother. What a useless position that was. Leo laughed, a harsh, ugly sound. 'I know how much it infuriated you that I was made heir—tell me, was it pride that kept you from begging Anders not to abdicate? Perhaps in time you would have accepted his bride, as long as it meant your son could be king.'

Nicholas's eyes narrowed to two slits blazing hatred and contempt, the only weapons he had. 'And now my grandson will be king instead,' he said coldly.

'If Parliament agrees to reinstate Anders posthumously.'

'They will.' Nicholas spoke with such certainty, and Leo knew he had reason to. Parliament did what the king wanted it to. He shook his head, the implications of Nicholas's pronouncement filtering through him.

He wouldn't be king. For six years he'd been the heir, serving the crown, serving Nicholas in attempt after attempt to show how worthy he was. Even if he didn't believe he was himself.

It had taken several years of honest living before the Press—and the people—started to believe in him, in the idea of him as king, but he'd won their trust. Their respect.

He'd never won the king's.

He was the son of a second son; he'd been a playboy, a reprobate, a rake. And deeming him even more unworthy were the feelings he'd locked inside himself, feelings he refused to consider or acknowledge because to do so would be to open a Pandora's box of emotions that might never be shut again.

And now it was going to be taken away, his life—and Christian's—irrevocably changed by the whim of an ill, old man. The twin demons of regret and guilt lashed him. He'd brought Phoebe straight into the lion's den—a pit of vipers! For if Christian was heir, there was no question of him returning to his life in New York...ever. And Nicholas would want Phoebe completely and utterly out of the way...out of the country, out of Christian's life, and he'd do whatever he could to achieve his goal.

And Leo...Leo had practically been his stooge. He'd thought he was serving the crown, but now he saw he'd only been serving the greedy whims of a vicious old man. He shook his head slowly, steeled his spine.

'If you're so determined to see the boy king, so be it,' he said coolly. 'I suppose you'd rather see the monarchy crumble to nothing than have me on the throne.' Nicholas's mouth tightened, but he didn't reply. 'But you won't get what you want by bulldozing over Christian's mother. As much as you might loathe her presence, she can't be bought or intimidated.'

'We'll see about—'

'She's American,' Leo cut across him coldly, 'and that boy is her whole world. She has no notion of royal duty as my mother did, and she won't be frightened or bullied the way my mother was.' Again he felt the old rage, the guilt and sorrow and regret. How could he have acted in such a way, putting Phoebe in the same utterly untenable position as his mother? How could he not have seen what was happening, what Nicholas was planning? Or had he just closed his mind to it, an act of bloody-minded will, because he was determined to do what he could to protect his crown?

Except the crown wasn't his any more.

Nicholas shrugged impatiently. 'I'll find a way—'

'No,' Leo cut him off, 'you won't.' Determination filled him, a cold sense of purpose that made him gaze directly, unflinchingly, at the king, allowing the old man to see his scorn. 'And if you want Christian to remain in this country, in the crown's protection, then you need a subtler method.' The smile he gave his uncle was cold and feral. 'From now on we'll do it my way.'

Phoebe rubbed her arms, fighting a rising sense of panic— near hysteria—as she paced the room, one of the palace's many salons. The doors, she knew, were locked. She'd tried them, rattled the handles helplessly, unable to believe they'd actually locked her away without a word of explanation…without her *son*.

She was a prisoner, and the realisation that she'd walked straight into this gilded jail made her choke. She'd trusted Leo—she hadn't even known she'd been doing so, he'd insinuated himself into her thoughts, her *heart* so insidiously—and now look where she was. Locked up like a criminal, and Christian—

She pressed a fist to her trembling lips and willed the panic to recede. She needed to be calm, to think clearly, rationally—

They couldn't just take him from her. Surely, *surely* in

this day and age, in the Western world, a mother couldn't be forcibly separated from her son—

Except she really had no idea what could happen, what the royal family could do. Lord, where *was* he? It had been half an hour, an endless thirty minutes. She resisted the urge to go to the door and rattle the knob once more, to pound and kick and scream until she was heard. Such antics would surely only weaken her position, and she needed to be *calm*—

A sound at the door had all sense of calm leaving her as she flew to it, her breath heaving in her chest. The door opened and Leo stood there, looking all too calm, all too unruffled—

'You lied!' Her voice came out close to a scream. 'They took him from me, and locked me in here—' She choked back a helpless sob.

Leo moved into the room, closing the door quietly behind him. 'I'm very sorry for what happened,' he said in a careful voice. 'That was never my intention.'

'Wasn't it?' Phoebe threw back at him. 'Somehow I have trouble believing you didn't know exactly—'

'I promise you, Phoebe, I didn't.' The intensity in his voice, the throbbing sincerity, made her still. She believed him, she hadn't been wrong to trust him, and the realisation—the *hope*—gave her comfort.

'Then what?' she asked, drawing in a steadying breath. 'The king acted on his own?'

'Basically, yes.' Leo thrust a hand into his pocket and strode to the window, gazing out at the cloudless blue sky, the palace courtyard glittering under a winter sun. Phoebe watched him, saw the tension in every taut line in his body, felt the anger simmering under his calm exterior. Perhaps he wasn't so unruffled after all.

'I thought the king wanted to see his grandson,' he said abruptly, his eyes on the sun-filled view outside. 'That's why I brought you here.'

Phoebe frowned, an uneasy confusion filling her. Even though Leo was still, his gaze on the palace courtyard, she sensed an anger in him…a restless darkness that she remembered from six years ago. 'Has something changed?' When Leo remained silent, gazing outside, she continued more forcefully, 'What does he want, Leo? Why did he separate us?'

'Because he's more interested in Christian than you,' Leo replied flatly.

Phoebe paced the floor again, rubbing her arms. 'I know that,' she said. 'I'd be an idiot not to. But…' All the unspoken fears—fears she couldn't afford to confess—clamoured up her throat, clawing their way out. Was the king going to seek custody, remove her from Christian's life completely? Her mother was right, she never should have come, she should have hired that dippy lawyer friend, something, *anything*—

'Phoebe.' Phoebe skidded to a halt, for suddenly Leo was there, his hands warm and steady on her shoulders, his eyes meeting, melting into hers. 'I'm not going to let anything happen, I promise.'

'How can you stop it? What's he planning, Leo?' She felt a hiccupy sob rise from her throat and she swallowed it back.

'I didn't realise…' Leo stopped, his lips pressed together, his face turning hard again.

'Realise what? Leo, what are you not telling me? What is the king planning?' Her voice rose with each question until it neared a shriek. 'Please,' she said in a whisper. 'Please be honest with me.'

Leo glanced down at her, and a surprising tenderness

softened his features. 'I will,' he told her. He raised one hand to brush her cheek with his knuckles, and it took all of Phoebe's strength to resist leaning into that caress. She wanted to lean into it, into him, to let someone share the burden of her fear and anxiety. She longed to trust Leo— he was the only one she could—and yet she was afraid that trusting him might be the biggest mistake of all. 'I will tell you,' he continued, 'but not now. You've only been in the country for little more than an hour, and I'm sure you want to see Christian.'

'Where is he?'

'Upstairs in the nursery, with my old governess. He's fine.'

Phoebe nodded. She still felt shaky and far too afraid, but Leo's words, his presence, his hand still cupping her cheek made her less so. Perhaps they shouldn't, but they did and she was even glad.

Leo smiled, his fingers drifting down her cheek to cup her chin. 'Tomorrow,' he told her, and bent his head so his lips brushed hers in the softest whisper of a kiss. He stepped back, his eyes widening slightly, and Phoebe wondered if he felt as dazed as she did. It had been the slightest kiss, their lips barely touching, and yet…! It had lit a fire of yearning in her body, that latent little spark igniting suddenly into a raging blaze.

'Leo…' she said, and heard the longing in her voice.

Leo touched her lips with his finger as if he was sealing the memory of his touch. 'We'll talk tomorrow.'

'*Tomorrow?*' She couldn't wait that long.

'You need rest.' Leo smiled, and Phoebe found herself fixated on his mouth, his lips so full, sculpted, *perfect*. Her own lips parted in memory and desire. 'I'll have someone see you to the nursery.'

'All right...' She knew she needed to process everything that had happened—including Leo's kiss—even though already she longed to see him again. Touch him again. Yet exhaustion was crashing over her in a numbing wave, and she knew Leo was right. She needed to see Christian, to restore some balance, some *sanity* to their lives. Still, as Leo turned away, clearly distracted, a prickle of unease rippled along her skin. What was he thinking, feeling and, more importantly—more frighteningly—what was he not saying?

The door clicked shut behind him and, alone in the salon, Leo swore aloud. His plan was working all too well. Phoebe trusted him, had responded to him—*mio Dio*, that kiss! He'd barely touched her, yet it hadn't mattered. That simple touch had set off an unstoppable response in both of them. He'd felt it before, all those years ago, and he certainly felt it now. His whole body ached with memory and desire, a longing to deepen that almost-kiss and join his body to hers...

No. Not yet. There was still more work to be done.

Guilt roiled within him, as bitter as bile. He was using Phoebe, using her with cold-hearted calculation. And if she discovered it...

He couldn't think that way. Couldn't afford to. The king's nefarious plans justified his own. This was the way it had to be; the only way it could be.

Numbly, Phoebe followed one of the royal servants to the top floor of the palace, where the nursery suite was located. She was met at the door by a pink-cheeked matron in a staid blue uniform.

'We've been waiting for you,' the nurse said, smiling with easy good humour.

'Where's my son?' Phoebe asked tersely, and Frances stepped aside to let her enter.

'He's right here, never you worry.'

'Mommy!' Christian stood up from his place on a colourful rug on the floor, bits of Lego scattered around him. 'Where have you been?'

Phoebe let out a shaky laugh of relief as she bent to scoop him into her arms. Christian squirmed, but she couldn't resist pressing a kiss to his head. 'I was talking to Leo,' she murmured, kissing him again. 'Are you all right?'

'Of course I am.' Christian wriggled away, returning to his Lego. 'I met the king.'

Phoebe sat back on her heels, her heart beating fast once more. 'Did you?' she asked lightly. 'Was he nice?'

'He was OK,' Christian said with a shrug, then glanced up. 'Why didn't you come with me?' His eyes widened, and Phoebe saw the fear lurking behind his boyish bravado.

'I wanted to,' she said carefully, 'but the king wanted some special time with you.'

Christian considered this as he placed another piece of Lego on the tower he was building. 'Oh,' he said, and just when Phoebe was about to let her breath out in relief of a confrontation avoided, he looked up with his clear, candid gaze. 'Why?'

'Time for elevenses!' Frances swept in with a tray of jam and bread as well as glasses of milk. 'You must be hungry, young man. Come and have a bite to eat.' Dutifully Christian sat at the table for his snack, and Phoebe rose, turning to Frances, who busied herself tidying up the toys.

'Thank you for taking care of him.'

'He's a lovely young man,' Frances replied. 'It was no trouble.'

'You've worked for the royal family for a long time,' Phoebe said slowly.

Frances nodded. 'Thirty-five years, since Leo was born. I took care of him as well as Anders.' Her expression sobered. 'Such a waste, that one. A loss.'

It was, sadly, a succinct and accurate summary of Anders's life. 'Yes,' Phoebe agreed quietly.

'You know, of course,' Frances continued with a nod and Phoebe started at her plain speaking. 'He couldn't keep his hand to anything.'

'No, I don't suppose he could.' Phoebe reached down to place a dog-eared book in the toy basket. 'You must have known them quite well, then? Anders…and Leo?'

Frances glanced up quickly, her expression shrewd before she shrugged and nodded. 'Yes, of course.'

Curiosity bit at Phoebe, made her want to ask questions. To know more, and even to understand. 'What were they like…together? Were they friends?'

Frances gave a short, derisive laugh. 'Friends? Those two? Not even for a moment.'

The abruptness and certainty of her answer made Phoebe ask, 'Why do you say that?'

'Because Anders was frightfully spoiled from the moment he was born. I did the best I could, but his parents doted on him dreadfully. He could do no wrong, and if he did…' she shrugged '…Leo was blamed.'

'Leo…?' Phoebe glanced quickly at Christian, but he was absorbed in a game he was playing quietly with himself at the table, his face smeared with jam. 'What do you mean?'

Frances sighed. 'It's not my place to say, but I can only imagine how difficult your position here must be, and the more information you have…' She stopped and shrugged again. 'Nicholas and Havard were brothers. It starts with them, you see. Nicholas hated Havard…he was jealous of him, of course. Everyone loved Havard. He was the younger brother, but I'm sure everyone wished he were the heir instead of Nicholas. He was handsome, charming, kind to everyone, while Nicholas was sour and spiteful. He couldn't help it, really. He was sickly as a child, pale and thin, while Havard was bursting with health. Or so I've been told…he was a husband and father by the time I met him. But it seemed that Nicholas had reason to be jealous, and that jealousy poisoned him.' Frances put the basket back on the shelf and brushed off her hands. 'Nicholas married first, a Danish woman, Johanna. She retired to Monaco when Anders abdicated, and died two years ago. But back then it seemed as if they might make a good match, until no children came. For ten years.' She shook her head. 'Ten long years. Meanwhile Havard married Ana, an Italian heiress, and had Leo practically nine months later. Nicholas was even more eaten up with jealousy. Everyone could see it, even me. I had been hired by then, to take care of Leo.'

'But Leo had no chance to be king,' Phoebe said. 'As the son of the younger son.'

'Well, that would be the case, if Nicholas didn't have any heirs. And Havard probably began to think his son might be king—he actually might be king—if Nicholas remained childless. There were rumours and whispers, as there always are, and no doubt they enraged Nicholas.'

Phoebe couldn't even imagine the tensions and rivalries that must have poisoned the royal household, the home Leo had grown up in. How had it affected him? *Changed* him? 'What happened then?' she asked in a whisper.

'Anders was born and Havard died,' Frances said simply, 'and everything changed.'

'How…?'

'Nicholas had an heir and Leo had nothing. His mother was sent back to Italy post-haste and Leo was treated like the poor relation. It's no wonder—' Frances stopped, shaking her head. 'But I shouldn't gossip like this, even if you deserve to know.'

Phoebe laid her hand on Frances's arm. 'Please,' she said, 'tell me.' She needed to know this history, needed to understand Leo.

Why…?

She couldn't even say, couldn't untangle the kaleidoscope of feelings tumbling through her. Fear, of course, was prevalent, but there was also compassion, wonder, hope.

Hope…?

That made no sense.

Phoebe turned back to Frances, who pursed her lips then gave a little shrug. 'It's no wonder he went off the rails a bit, that's all,' she finally said.

'The Playboy Prince,' Phoebe murmured, and Frances nodded.

'Exactly.' Christian rose from the table, gleefully holding out his jam-covered hands. 'Come here, love,' Frances said, bustling over to him, clearly glad to have a reason to end the conversation with Phoebe. 'Let's get you washed off.'

Christian went for a wash off with Frances, and Phoebe was left alone in the nursery with its high sashed windows and pale oak floor. She sank onto a sofa, her mind spinning. She felt she understood Leo so much more now…why he'd been such a playboy, so cynical, and why he'd changed. For he *had* changed, she thought. The unneeded spare had become the heir, the prince who would be king, and duty rather than desire—a lust for pleasure—drove him now.

Yet could she really think she knew—understood— Leo? She *wanted* to know him, to trust him, even to like him. She touched her finger to her lips, and knew she wanted more than to like him. Desire, consuming, endless, flooded her.

Yet was it wise—safe—to trust such a man? To desire him? Was Leo truly being kind, or just softening her for the kill? Did he intend to take away her son? Phoebe swallowed back the acid taste of fear. She didn't, Phoebe realised, really know Leo at all.

'Mommy!' Christian came back into the nursery, his face brightening as he turned to the door. 'Leo!'

Phoebe froze. The room, the whole world seemed to stand still as she turned slowly. Leo stood in the doorway, smiling, natural, and entirely at ease, his relaxed stance starting to dispel her fears of moments before even as her heart rate kicked up at the sight of him. She could almost taste the memory of his lips on hers, inhale his scent...

'Hello, Christian,' he said. 'I thought I'd come and see how you are.'

'There are lots of toys here,' Christian told him matter-of-factly, 'but some of them are old.'

'Ah.' Leo's laughing eyes met Phoebe's over Christian. 'Those would be mine.'

Phoebe let out a little bubble of surprised laughter, and Leo smiled back, his eyes so very warm on hers, melting her fears clear away. *If only I could stay in the same room with this man*, she thought suddenly, *and have him smile at me forever*.

Strange, when his smile had used to scare her. Years ago it had been so cold, so cruel and callous and calculating. Yet now she basked in the sunlight and warmth of Leo's smile and wondered how she could have ever doubted that he'd changed. At that moment, it seemed so wonderfully obvious.

'I thought,' Leo said, coming farther into the nursery, 'that you could have dinner in your rooms tonight. Since you're most likely tired.'

'I'm not—' Christian began and Leo's eyes met Phoebe's once more.

'I think,' he said softly, 'it would be best.'

Phoebe nodded slowly. 'Thank you,' she said slowly. The farther away she stayed from King Nicholas, the better.

'And tomorrow,' Leo continued, 'I thought we'd go ice-skating. Every year a rink is created in Njardvik's main square, by the biggest Christmas tree you've ever seen. It is quite a sight.'

Christian cocked his head, clearly sceptical. 'Bigger than the tree at the Rockefeller Center?'

'Hmm.' Leo pursed his lips. 'I'm not sure about that, actually. But the rink is most certainly bigger.'

Christian nodded in acceptance, excitement lighting his eyes, and Phoebe touched Leo's sleeve. 'Leo—' she said quietly, and he turned to her, his gaze warming her once more.

'There will be time for us to talk later, Phoebe,' Leo said softly, so only she could hear. 'When we are rested…and alone. I promise.'

Alone. And what would happen when they were alone? Nerves and something else—something wonderful and intoxicating—fluttered deep in Phoebe's belly. 'And when will that be?' she asked, knowing Leo could hear the longing in her voice. Desire had made her transparent.

'Soon.' His voice was a caress. 'I promise.'

Phoebe nodded, knowing she would have to leave it at that, even though her mind seethed with questions and her body ached with unfulfilled yearning. 'All right,' she murmured, and a few minutes later he excused himself to return to work. Phoebe took Christian back to their suite and, despite many mighty protests, he quite promptly fell asleep.

Phoebe remained awake, restless, anxious, both her body and mind unsated, unfulfilled. And yet, even so, amidst all the turbulent uncertainty coursing through her, she felt hopeful as well. She gazed out at the palace gardens, the bare branches of the trees stark against the darkening sky, the grounds shrouded in winter, and wondered what on earth she had to hope for.

Yet it was there, deep inside her, a tightly furled bud ready to burst open and bloom in the light of day, in the warmth of a man's smile, in the memory of his kiss, in the belief—naïve and misplaced as it might be—that she could trust him, that perhaps he could be a friend…or perhaps—*perhaps*—even something more.

'The king is expecting me,' Leo coolly informed the aide standing guard outside Nicholas's bedchamber. The aide moved aside and Leo let himself into the darkened room.

King Nicholas sat up in bed, an ornately carved four-poster, several pillows piled behind him and the coverlet folded over his knees.

'Well?' he demanded in a rasp. 'Did it work?'

'Did what work?' Leo asked laconically, and Nicholas gave a growl of impatience.

'Whatever this plan of yours is, to get the girl out of the way.'

'Oh, yes,' Leo replied. He propped one shoulder against one of the bedposts as he surveyed Nicholas's frail form. 'It's working.'

'I don't see why we couldn't just buy her off,' Nicholas grumbled. 'Or run a smear campaign—'

'Trashing her in the tabloids would hardly benefit your heir,' Leo pointed out sardonically, 'and I told you, she can't be bought.'

'And as I told you, everyone can be bought, Leo,' the old man said. He paused, his eyes glinting with malice. 'Your own mother's price was fifty thousand.' He paused, clearly savouring Leo's surprise. 'American.'

Leo froze, his gaze sweeping over his uncle in icy assessment. He didn't want to believe what he'd just heard; he wanted to call the king a liar. Desperately. Surely his mother wouldn't have accepted money in the place of her son. Yet, looking at Nicholas's sleek smile of satisfaction, he knew he wasn't lying. His mother had accepted cash to abandon her child to the royal family and their machinations, and clearly Nicholas had been waiting for such a moment as this to tell him so.

He felt a wave of icy shock at the realisation, and underneath a deeper hurt he couldn't bear to probe. He snapped his unfocused gaze back to his uncle and smiled lazily.

'At least she got something out of it, then,' he said in a drawl, and Nicholas let out a raspy laugh.

'So what is your plan with this American?'

Leo smiled coldly. It was a sign of the old man's unbelievable arrogance that he trusted Leo to carry out his bidding even now, when he'd told him he would no longer be his heir. He'd cut him out of the succession as ruthlessly as if he'd wielded scissors, yet Nicholas didn't doubt or question Leo for a moment. He simply wasn't accustomed to disobedience. The only one who'd dared to go against him in a moment of childish folly had been Anders, and look where it had got him…abdicated, exiled, dead. A waste of a life. Leo swallowed back the rush of guilt such thoughts always caused him and turned to address his uncle.

'There's no need for you to know the details,' he said coolly. 'I'm carrying it out and it will deal with…the in-convenience…in due course.'

'Inconvenience.' Nicholas snickered. 'Yes, she is that.' He shifted in his bed, adjusting the pile of pillows behind him. 'Well, as long as you take care of it, and soon.'

'Oh, yes,' Leo assured him, his voice terribly bland. 'I'll have it dealt with by tomorrow night.'

'Good.' Nicholas pulled the coverlet up over his chest, a cough rattling in his bony chest. For a moment Leo felt a flicker of sympathy for the old bastard; even he couldn't defeat Father Time. 'Now I'm tired,' Nicholas said. 'I'll speak to you in the morning.'

'Of course.' Leo sketched a short, mocking bow before leaving his uncle's bedroom.

Back in his own suite of rooms, Leo automatically went to the drinks tray before, with a muttered curse, he turned away. He unlocked the French doors leading to a terrace and stepped outside.

The wrought-iron railing was cold under his bare hands, the night air freezing and sharp, like a knife to the lungs. Stars glittered in a mercilessly black sky, the moon no more than a pale sliver of silver. In the distance the harbour gleamed blackly in the moonlight, and Leo smelled the promise of snow in the frigid, damp air.

He cursed aloud.

He'd never felt so trapped, so backed into a corner, as

he did right then, and the king didn't even realise. No one did. He had to protect Phoebe. He had to protect the crown. And he could see only one solution. A solution that required him to manipulate and use Phoebe with cold precision.

He had to make Phoebe his wife.

It would save her, but it would also condemn her. Condemn her to the politics of the royal family, a life she didn't choose in a foreign country, a loveless marriage to him.

There was passion between them, Leo knew—oh, how he knew; he still felt it in every restless, unsatisfied sinew and limb. He felt it every time he saw her, uncoiling deep within him, radiating out to his fingertips that ached to touch her, brush the creaminess of her skin, the softness of her lips, her hair…

It was that latent sense of need that had given him the idea in the first place, and yet was it enough? Would Phoebe agree? Accept…?

And would she hate him when she knew…discovered what he'd done, what kind of man he was?

Would it even—ever—come to that?

Leo closed his eyes. Phoebe was a good woman, a better woman, perhaps, than even his own mother, who, he now knew, had given in to if not greed, then desperation. Thirty years after the fact he could feel pity—despite the pain—for a woman who had been so bullied by the royal family she'd allowed herself to be bought off.

Yet Phoebe didn't let herself be bullied or bought; despite her fear, she'd stayed strong. She was a good woman, Leo thought with a pang of guilty regret. Far too good for him.

A cold wind blew over him, rustling the tree branches, making him shiver. Suppressing another curse, Leo resolutely turned and went back inside.

CHAPTER SEVEN

PHOEBE awoke to a pearly pink sky and dawn streaking its pale fingers along the floor. Next to her Christian lay sprawled across the bed. He'd had a restless night and sometime between midnight and dawn Phoebe had brought him into bed with her.

Now she lay still, enjoying a moment of peaceful solitude even as the memories and implications of yesterday trickled slowly through her.

They were in Amarnes. Nicholas might very well want custody of her son. Leo had kissed her.

She rolled off the bed, carefully extracting herself from the rumpled covers so as not to wake Christian. The sun was rising now, a pale sliver of yellow above the mountains, turning their snow-capped peaks to the colour of cream. A glance at the clock told her it was already after eight o'clock; in November the sun didn't rise until quite late in this part of the world.

Hurriedly, Phoebe washed and dressed. Today they were going ice-skating with Leo. And despite all her fears and anxieties, the terror that Nicholas would find a way to take Christian from her and, even worse, that Leo might aid him, she found herself looking forward to the outing with absurd excitement.

An hour later they were leaving the palace, just the three of them, bundled against the chilly wind blowing in from the sea.

'What, no entourage?' Phoebe asked as they simply strolled through the palace gates. 'No guards?'

'Amarnes is a small country,' Leo replied with a shrug. 'Very safe. And I think I can take on any comers.' His wry smile as he flexed one arm made Phoebe laugh aloud. She needed this, she realised. She needed to laugh, to let go, to enjoy a day apart, a day just for pleasure…with Leo.

Next to her, Christian was practically dancing in excitement. So much for the Rockefeller Center, Phoebe thought wryly. He obviously thought this was much more fun.

She'd certainly agree with that.

The sun was just emerging behind some ribbony white clouds as they entered the city's main square. Phoebe's last visit to Njardvik had been such a blur that she now found herself looking around in genuine interest. The square was surrounded by tall, narrow townhouses painted in varying pastel shades, elegant and colourful.

In the middle of the square, now strung with fairy lights, an ice rink had been formed, sparkling with sunlight. A Christmas tree decorated in red and gold, at least forty feet high, towered over the rink. Even Christian was impressed by its size, and declared it better than the tree at the Rockefeller Center.

'I'm so relieved,' Leo told him with a little smile.

They fetched skates from a hut erected near the rink, and then sat on a rough wooden bench to put them on. Phoebe saw the way the people—the man who rented them the skates, the red-cheeked woman who sold *pebber nodder*, the little shortbread cookies flavoured with cinnamon—looked at him. Spoke to him. She saw and heard respect, admiration, even affection. Leo, Phoebe realised, had won his people over.

The thought made her glad.

'Have you skated much?' Leo asked with an arched brow, and Phoebe smiled, suddenly mischievous.

'A bit.' She tightened the laces on her skates. 'What about you?'

'A bit as well,' Leo replied.

'I fall a lot,' Christian confided. He stretched out his legs for Leo to lace up his skates. Phoebe watched the simple sight of Leo doing up her son's skates and felt her heart both constrict and expand all at once. There was something so *right* about this, and it scared her. It was all too easy to imagine them as a family, to imagine this was more than just a day's outing. To imagine—and want—this to be real.

'There.' Leo stood up, reaching a hand down to Christian, which the little boy took with easy trust. He held out his other hand to Phoebe, and after the briefest of hesitations she took it. They both wore gloves, yet even so it felt all too good— too right and too wonderful—for his hand to clasp hers.

They walked awkwardly on their skates to the rink and Christian's bravado faltered at the sight of the sheer ice. Skating backwards with long, gliding movements, Leo took the boy's hands and helped him move along. Phoebe watched from the side as they skated around the rink. Leo had skated more than a bit, she thought wryly. He skated backwards with effortless ease, helping Christian along, encouraging him with ready smiles and praise. Christian beamed back, delighted when he was finally able to let go of Leo's hands and skate for a few wobbly feet by himself.

Leo skated towards Phoebe, who remained leaning against the rink wall.

'You're good,' she said and he gave a modest shrug.

'Growing up in Amarnes…all children learn to skate.' He gave her a little smile. 'Are you going to get out on the ice?' His eyes glinted with humour. 'You're not afraid, are you?'

'Me? Afraid?'

'You said you'd only skated a bit…'

'So I did,' Phoebe agreed, and then pushed off the wall. She wasn't able to see the expression on Leo's face as she glided to the centre of the rink, did a graceful figure-of-eight before spinning in a dizzying circle, one leg stretched out in a perfect right angle.

'Way to go, Mom!' Christian crowed, then turned to Leo. 'She used to skate a lot.'

'So it would appear,' Leo murmured, and Phoebe, skating back, couldn't help but grin.

'I took figure-skating lessons for five years. I had dreams of being the next big star, actually.'

'And what happened?'

Phoebe smiled wryly. 'I wasn't *that* good.'

'Better than me,' Leo told her. 'And you don't need to look so smug,' he added as she leaned against the wall once more. 'I was looking forward to giving you lessons.'

'Perhaps it should be the other way round,' Phoebe replied, and he laughed aloud.

'Or perhaps,' he murmured for only her ears, 'we should have lessons in some other…field of interest.'

Suddenly Phoebe was breathless, the camaraderie of the moment replaced by something deeper, needier and more elemental.

She wanted him. She wanted to touch him, kiss him, to feel every bit of his skin, his hair, his mouth and eyes—his body. She wanted his body inside her, wanted to feel him move against her—

She turned away, afraid her thoughts—her need—would be reflected in her eyes. Leo was so adept at reading her emotions, and she wasn't ready for him to know this.

Although perhaps he already did. Perhaps he'd always known it, from the moment he'd first touched her all those years ago, and she'd felt as if he'd reached right inside to her soul. Perhaps he had…perhaps her ill-fated marriage had never had a chance from that moment.

Perhaps, Phoebe thought hazily, it had always been Leo.

'Aren't we going to skate some more?' Christian demanded, and Leo reached for his hands.

'Yes, we are,' he said as he started skating backwards again, Christian following him. 'And then we're going to get some hot chocolate.'

They skated for another half-hour before the cold defeated them, and they returned their skates.

'There's a café near here,' Leo said, 'with the most delicious hot chocolate.' He smiled at Christian. 'With whipped cream.'

The air was sharp with brine and damp with cold as they left the rink, even though the sun was shining.

They walked in easy silence down the narrow streets to the promised café, a small, wood-panelled room in the front of a townhouse, its scarred oak tables and chairs relics from another century.

The owner hurried towards them, all welcoming smiles and excited chatter, which Leo, looking almost discomfited, waved away. Within seconds they were seated at a more private table in the back, scarves and mittens shed, and coats hung over their chairs.

One of the waiters brought Christian a colouring book and some crayons, and he was soon hard at work. Phoebe took the opportunity to study Leo, her heart—and something else—lurching at the sight of him. A few stray snow-flakes glittered in his hair, and his cheeks were bright with cold. She could see the glint of stubble on his jaw, and it made her ache to reach out and touch the bristles, compare the feel of it to the softness of his lips…

On the table she curled her hand into a fist, deter-mined—for the moment—to resist the impulse. Leo glanced at her, amusement quirking his mouth.

'You look as if you're deep in thought,' he said. 'Or per-haps working out a difficult maths problem. What are you thinking about?'

Phoebe had no intention of telling him the nature of her thoughts. She smiled and began to shrug, surprising them both when she suddenly said, 'You *have* changed.'

Leo stilled, his long, brown fingers flat on the table. He didn't quite look at her as he asked lightly, 'Have I?'

'Yes,' Phoebe said more forcefully. 'You're not… you're not…'

'A reckless, womanising playboy any more?' he asked, his voice still light, but she heard—felt—the darkness underneath. The same emotion she'd felt from him all those years ago, a kind of pain or sorrow.

'No,' she said quietly. 'But it's more than that.'

Leo opened his menu and scanned the pages. 'How in-triguing,' he murmured, but Phoebe could tell he wanted to deflect the conversation from himself, and she won-dered why.

A waiter returned with mugs of creamy cocoa, and Phoebe dipped her spoon in the frothy confection. 'So did you put your partying days behind you when you realised you'd become king?'

Something flashed in Leo's eyes—something bleak and angry—and then he shrugged. 'Something like that. I told you before, didn't I, some things can be sordid and boring?'

She felt a flicker of disappointment. 'So the party scene just got old?'

'It always does.'

Christian looked up from his mug of hot chocolate, his entire face flecked with whipped cream. 'What does sordid mean?'

And that, Phoebe thought, was a signal to change the conversation if there ever was one. Yet she was curious, far too curious, about Leo. About his childhood, about his change of heart, about the man he was now. A man, she realised with both alarm and excitement, that she could more than like. A man she could love.

They finished their hot chocolate in comfortable silence, before Leo said they should return to the palace. 'You, young man, look tired.'

'I am not!' Christian protested with five-year-old indignation.

'Well,' Leo relented, 'perhaps your mother is. Maybe I could show you the palace games room while she has a nap? I play a mean game of air hockey.' He glanced at Phoebe in silent query, and she gave a little nod. A nap sounded heavenly.

Outside the café they came across one of Njardvik's little Christmas markets, a narrow street lined on both sides with stalls, each one strung with lights and offering various handicrafts, baked goods and Christmas ornaments.

'Are these all Santa Clauses?' Phoebe asked as she examined a row of carved wooden figures, each with a long white beard and red cap.

'Santas, no. They're *nissen*,' Leo replied. 'Sort of like Santa—but a *nisse* is a bit of a trickier fellow.'

'Trickier?'

'Yes, he was originally a protector of family farms. But he might steal the cows' hay to give to the horses—that sort of thing. Now he's become a bit more like Santa. On Christmas Eve someone dresses up as a *nisse* and brings presents, asking if there are any good children.'

'Did someone do that for you as a child? In the palace?' Phoebe asked suddenly. She pictured Anders and Leo at Christmas, waiting for the *nisse*. Knowing what she did, she could imagine Anders vying for all the attention while Leo stood in the shadows, watching.

'Oh, yes.' Leo's expression was strangely shuttered. 'Always.'

'And what did you answer?' Phoebe asked, keeping her voice light. 'Were you a good child?' She meant to sound light, teasing, but instead the question sounded serious. Leo's mouth stretched in a smile and he put the *nisse* back on the shelf. 'Oh, yes,' he said, 'of course I was.'

Yet Phoebe could only imagine what he wasn't saying, what memories he was keeping to himself. Ignored, neglected, a virtual orphan. He might have been a good child, she thought, but she doubted he had been a happy one. She glanced back at the *nisse*; the look on the little statue's face suddenly seemed closer to a sneer.

They left the Christmas market and began to walk back to the palace, Leo leading them down the city's narrow cobbled streets, his hand easily linked with Christian's. Phoebe trailed a few steps behind, watching them, thinking how much like a family—a father and son—they looked.

What if Leo had been Christian's father, instead of Anders? What if all those years ago, she had met him first? What if they'd fallen in love?

Useless questions, Phoebe knew, and ones she couldn't

possibly answer. The past was the past; it had been written, finished. The present was intriguing enough.

And as for the future…

What could there possibly be between her and Leo, the heir to the country's throne? She'd been considered an unsuitable candidate for queen six years ago, and she doubted anything had changed on that score.

Besides, wasn't she getting a little ahead of herself? All Leo had done was kiss her, and such a little brush of a kiss it barely counted.

Except it hadn't *felt* little.

And yet in two weeks she would be returning home with Christian—at least, that was what she wanted, what she'd hoped for. Her fears about the king's plans and intentions still gnawed nervously at her insides. Even so, amidst the fear and the uncertainty, she now felt a longing for these two weeks to never end.

It was working, Leo thought grimly, his hand still loosely clasped with Christian's. With half an ear he listened to the boy chatter on about some kind of toy—a robot or a dinosaur?—as his own mind spun in circles. He'd had a plan, he'd carried it out, and it was clearly a success.

Phoebe was falling in love with him.

So why did that make him feel so miserable?

Because I don't deserve it…I don't deserve any of it, I never did or will…

He pushed the thoughts away, the tormented voices of his conscience, his memory. He couldn't afford to have either. He needed to focus, to keep working towards his goal. And even if Phoebe hated him, even if she discovered the truth, he knew he was doing only what he had to.

For Phoebe's sake.

* * *

Phoebe gazed at herself in the mirror, amazed at the trans-formation. That afternoon several gowns had been sent to her room with instructions she choose one to wear that evening. A single card had been inserted among the folds of tissue paper, with a single sentence upon it, written in a bold scrawl: *Have dinner with me.*

Her heart hammered in anticipation and her nerves jangled as she undid the dresses from their folds of paper and hung them on the door, gazing at each one in turn. What to wear to dinner tonight? Dinner alone with Leo. Now finally he would explain what he knew of the king's plans, yet Phoebe found she could barely think of that.

All she could think of, her body's insistent needs drowning out her mind's, was being alone with Leo. What would happen? What would he do? What would *she* do?

'Which one should I wear?' she asked Christian, who was sprawled on the bed, watching a children's show in Danish with an expression of endearing perplexity.

He glanced up at her, frowning at the sight of the clothes. 'Are those dresses?' he asked and Phoebe laughed, reaching over to ruffle his hair. Christian promptly ducked out of the way and returned to watching the television.

'Yes, silly. And can you actually understand that show at all?'

'I saw it back at home,' Christian replied with a shrug and Phoebe rolled her eyes.

'Come on, sport. Help me out here.'

With a long-suffering sigh, Christian turned away from the TV once more. He glanced at the three gowns, his brow furrowed. 'The silver one.'

'You think?' Phoebe reached out to stroke the slippery, silky material. It was a bit pathetic, getting fashion advice from a five-year-old, but she needed to talk to someone.

To let out some of this energy, this excitement bubbling away inside of her.

'Yeah.' Christian had clearly had enough of fashion talk, for he turned back to the show, which featured a talking lion that happened to be friends with a zebra. 'It's the same colour as my robot.'

'And that's as good a reason as any,' Phoebe murmured, slipping the dress off its hanger. She went into the bathroom to change, and the dress's material flowed over her like liquid silver. It was deceptive in its simplicity, two skinny straps and a bodice decorated with tiny jet beads that ended in a swirl of shimmery silk around her ankles.

'It matches your eyes,' Christian said when she came out to show him. She laughed, twirling around, feeling beautiful.

'How kind of you to notice.'

'Did you bring your hair stuff?'

Christian knew how she disliked her curly hair that always tended to frizz. When she had time, she used a special hair serum and blow-dried it straight. 'No, I didn't,' she said with some reluctance. 'Leo will just have to take me as I am.'

'You're eating with Leo?' Christian asked, astute as ever, and Phoebe flushed.

'Yes, we're having dinner together while you get to be with Frances.'

Christian narrowed his eyes. 'Are you going to marry him?'

'Christian!' Phoebe stared at her son in shock. 'What makes you think such a thing?'

He shrugged. 'He's nice and I don't have a dad,' he said simply. Phoebe's heart ached.

'I didn't realise you wanted one,' she said quietly, and

Christian gave her a look that clearly said such a thought was incredibly stupid. And wasn't it? Phoebe asked herself. No matter how many friends she surrounded Christian with, no matter how much love she showered him with, didn't he still want a father?

Didn't he still need one?

And could Leo be it—him?

Whoa, Phoebe told herself. You're getting way, way ahead of the game. Leo had merely asked her to dinner. He'd only kissed her once. And yet...and yet...

She wanted so much more. She was ready for so much more. For the last five years she'd put her own romantic life on hold, for Christian's sake. Building her business and caring for her son had been enough.

Now it wasn't.

Now she wanted more. She wanted Leo.

At seven o'clock Phoebe took Christian up to the nursery and was met at the door by a smiling Frances.

'My, don't we look nice tonight!' she exclaimed, taking Christian by the hand. She winked at Phoebe. 'You're not going on a date, are you?'

'Just dinner,' Phoebe murmured, blushing. What was with everybody? she wondered. Were her hopes so transparent?

'Well, enjoy yourself,' Frances replied comfortably. 'I'm sure we will.'

Leaving Christian in the nurse's capable hands, Phoebe made her way downstairs. A servant directed her not to the main dining room, but to a private salon in the back of the palace.

The servant opened the door, disappearing quickly and quietly before Phoebe had even properly entered. And then she stopped, for the room, with its fireplace and dancing shadows, the rich wood panelling and the heavy velvet curtains the colour of wine, was sumptuous and beautiful and reminded her of the room at the consulate.

For just as before there was Leo standing by the fireplace, dressed in an immaculate suit, his hair brushed back from his forehead and curling on his collar. He looked amazing, seductive and beautiful and she wanted him more than anything she'd ever wanted in her life.

For, while the room seemed so similar to that room at the consulate, the mood was different. She was different…and so was Leo. Gone was the fear, the outrage, the anger. She came into the room smiling.

'Did I really need to wear a formal gown?'

'I was hoping you'd choose the grey one.'

His words caused a prickly heat of awareness to creep along her arms and flush her face and bare shoulders. 'You selected those gowns?'

Leo arched one eyebrow. 'Are you questioning my taste?'

Laughing a little, Phoebe shook her head. 'No. They were all beautiful.'

Leo started forward, towards her. 'But the grey one matches your eyes.'

'That's what Christian said.'

'Smart boy.' He stopped in front of her, close enough for her to touch him if she reached her hand out and yet still too far away.

Phoebe's heart bumped in her chest; she felt as if Leo could see it through the tissue-thin fabric of her dress. She stared at him, unspeaking, helpless, because she had so many things to say and she didn't know how to begin. 'I'm hungry.'

Leo's lips curved in a smile and Phoebe flushed. She

hadn't meant to say that, but the words had come out anyway. 'So am I,' he said, and Phoebe knew he wasn't just talking about food.

He reached out one hand to touch hers, lacing their fingers together, and drew her deeper into the room. His touch created an instant and overwhelming response, so her legs felt like butter, soft and melting as she practically swayed towards him.

'Leo…'

'Let me pour you a glass of wine.'

But she didn't need wine; she felt drunk already, dizzy and light and free. 'All right,' she whispered. She watched as he poured from the bottle already opened on the sideboard and then handed her a crystal glass, raising his own in a toast. 'To tonight,' he said, and the words were surely a promise of what was to come.

Phoebe drank, letting the rich liquid slide down her throat and fire her belly. She felt floaty and weightless, suspended in the moment, unable to think or care about anything else. She knew, absolutely knew, she shouldn't feel this way. Wasn't this evening meant to be about the future? About the king and his plans? About what Leo knew? Yet all the questions she'd meant to ask, all the answers she'd meant to demand, seemed to float away to nothing, meaningless in the face of the consuming desire she felt for this man.

'Shall we eat?' Leo asked, and Phoebe nodded, for, though she'd claimed to be hungry, surely the meal was simply something to be got through, to be endured before the rest of the evening began.

She moved to the table, her gown swishing sensuously against her bare legs, and sat down.

'Please. Allow me.' Leo set down his wine glass and

took the heavy linen napkin from the table, unfolding it with a flourish and then spreading it on her lap, his fingers brushing and even lingering on her thighs. Phoebe closed her eyes, savouring the caress.

Leo moved to the other side of the table and sat down, and Phoebe forced herself to open her eyes, to act normal. To feel normal. His knee nudged hers under the table, a subtle, steady pressure that had fiery sensation flooding through her once more.

This had to stop. It had to *begin.*

'Something smells delicious,' Phoebe said.

'Indeed.' Leo lifted the lids on several silver chafing-dishes; a tantalising aroma of rosemary and lemon wafted from a dish of roasted chicken. Leo placed some on her plate, along with fresh asparagus and new potatoes. He handed her a basket of bread; the rolls were soft and flaky.

Yet Phoebe couldn't taste it, or at least the taste was overwhelmed by her other senses. The feel of Leo's knee against hers, the sight of him, the *scent* of him.

She couldn't take any more, she thought almost frantically. She was burning up, her body aching and restless—

'Phoebe,' Leo said quietly, putting down his fork, 'the king wishes to make Christian his heir.'

The words didn't make sense. They penetrated Phoebe's haze of desire like buzzing flies, circling in her fevered brain. *The king wants to make Christian his heir...his heir...his heir...*

'But...that's impossible.' The words felt thick and clumsy on her tongue, and she blinked, struggling to find clarity amidst her body's clamouring needs. 'Anders abdicated. Christian has no right—'

'The king has decided otherwise.' Leo gazed at her

directly, watched her carefully. Did he think she was going to throw a fit? To scream and shriek and cry?

For now the lovely fog of desire was burning off under the cruel light of dawning realisation. If Christian was the king's heir, then he would be king one day. Of Amarnes. He would live his life here, his life would be forfeit to the crown, and Phoebe—what role would she have?

The answer was obvious. None. She rose from the table on legs made shaky now by fear. '*This* has been his plan?' she asked sickly, though she knew, of course, it was. 'All along?'

'Yes…although I did not know it.'

She shot Leo a dark glance. 'No, you wouldn't, would you? If Christian is named heir, then you won't be—'

'King. No.' Leo spoke with no intonation, no inflection, no emotion at all. Phoebe turned around to stare at him helplessly. What was he thinking right now? Feeling? She had no idea, no clue, and it scared her. The heady hope of the last twenty-four hours, brimming as they had been with possibility, suddenly seemed ludicrous. False. Who *was* this man?

'Are you disappointed?' she asked and Leo shrugged one shoulder.

'I could hardly say I did not feel some disappointment at the news. But if the king wishes it, there is little I can say or do about the matter.'

'And what can I do?' Phoebe demanded. 'I don't want Christian to be king!' She thought of her mother's lawyer friend. How did you contest a line of succession? Was it even possible?

'I wouldn't go down that route, Phoebe,' Leo said quietly, and she heard a raw note of compassion in his voice. 'It won't get you anywhere.'

'But how can he…? This isn't a dictatorship—don't you have a parliament or something—?'

'Yes, and I'm afraid they'll do what Nicholas says. He is—and has been—a strong ruler.'

Just like that, Phoebe thought, too shocked and sick at heart even to feel angry. Just like that, Nicholas could change everything, everyone's lives.

'So what am I supposed to do?' She finally asked brokenly. 'Just…roll over? Accept this?' Her voice rose and her hands fisted at her sides. 'Leo, he can't become king! Frances told me how awful the royal family—your family—is!' she continued wildly, driven by desperation. 'All the jealousies and rivalries—your own mother was sent away!'

Leo stilled, his face now utterly blank. 'Yes, she was.'

'And is that what's going to happen to me?' Phoebe demanded. 'Is the king going to send me away, or will he just try to buy me off again?'

'No,' Leo replied calmly. 'He wanted to buy you off in New York, but I never made the offer.'

'What…?' The single word came out in a hiss.

'A million euros,' Leo clarified dispassionately. 'But I knew as soon as I saw you, Phoebe, that you would never take such an offer, and I would never make one.' He paused, turning his head so his face was averted from her, cast in shadow. 'You were right, my mother was sent away when I was six. When Anders was born. My father died the same year, and Nicholas couldn't wait to get rid of me. Or at least put me in my proper place.' He laughed shortly. 'Of course, he couldn't do so without first getting rid of my mother. She wasn't needed any more, and Nicholas wanted a clear playing field.' Leo let out a long, ragged breath. 'He bought her off.'

Phoebe's eyes widened in shock; she still couldn't see Leo's face, but she could feel the pain emanating from him in sorrowful waves. 'Leo, I'm sorry.'

'I saw her only a handful of times after that, and she died when I was sixteen. She had a weak chest.' He turned his head, met her gaze. 'So I could hardly let the same happen to you,' he continued, and Phoebe saw the bleak honesty in his eyes. 'Even though I was tempted.'

'Tempted...?'

'You were an inconvenience, remember?' Leo gave her the ghost of a smile. 'At least, I thought of you as one until I saw you again.'

Her heart bumped painfully against her ribs. She wanted to ask Leo what he meant, wanted to hope, *needed* to, but the future—Christian's future—was too overwhelming. 'So what can we do?' she whispered. 'We can't— I can't—' She stopped, took a breath, and started again in a stronger voice. 'I won't be bought, and I won't leave Christian.'

'I know.' Leo smiled, his mouth curling upwards in a way that made Phoebe's insides tingle with awareness, with anticipation. 'I have another solution.' He paused, and in that second's silence Phoebe felt as if the room—the whole world—became hushed in expectation, as if everything had led to this moment, this question, this possibility. As if she already *knew*. Leo took a step towards her, his hand outstretched. 'Phoebe,' he said, 'you can become my wife.'

CHAPTER EIGHT

PHOEBE stared at him in wordless disbelief. She'd been expecting...something—and yet this? Marriage? 'Your *what*?'

'My wife.' Leo's smile widened. 'It's really very simple.'

'Is it?' she asked incredulously, and Leo took another step towards her.

'Of course. If you marry me, you can stay in Amarnes. More importantly, you can stay in Christian's life. You'll have a place, guaranteed.'

'As Queen of Amarnes.'

'I'm afraid not,' Leo corrected softly. 'It'll be back to the Duchy of Larsvik, I'm afraid.'

'Oh, well.' Phoebe tried to laugh; the sound that emerged was something between a hiccup and a ragged sob. 'I suppose I'd have to settle for being a duchess.'

'Sorry to disappoint,' Leo said, his mouth quirking, but she saw the darkness in his eyes. This was no joking matter.

'Leo...'

'Is there any reason why you should refuse?'

She shook her head. There were too many reasons to

name, and yet there was also a terrible desire to simply say *yes*. How could she do something so impractical, so *insane*? 'What is this?' she finally managed. 'Some kind of pity proposal?'

'Do I seem the kind of man to marry someone out of pity?' Leo asked, arching one eyebrow.

'You don't seem the kind of man to marry at all.'

Leo gave a small nod of acknowledgement. 'Perhaps, but I have always accepted that I will have to settle down one day. It is expected.'

'Is that supposed to make me feel better?'

'It is simply the truth. Besides, our marriage will help stabilise the monarchy. A child king…'

'Nicholas isn't dead yet,' Phoebe reminded him, and Leo gave a little shrug.

'And Christian is only five. I would not want to see him at the mercy of a regent who did not have his best interests in mind.'

'And you would?' Phoebe asked. Leo regarded her levelly.

'Of course.'

It was too much to take in. Ruler, regent, kings and queens and even a duchy—she felt as if she'd stumbled into a fairy tale.

Was this the happy ending?

'So.' Leo waited, hands spread wide, for Phoebe's answer.

She didn't want to state the obvious, but she knew she had to. 'We don't love each other.'

Leo hesitated, and when he spoke his voice was careful. 'No, but we've certainly enjoyed each other's company these last few days. Who knows what could happen in time?'

Was he actually saying he might come to love her? Phoebe wondered, her heart swelling with awful hope. This was such an insane idea. She couldn't marry Leo. A few days ago she hadn't even liked him. She'd hated him, despised and mistrusted him, the sardonic, cynical Playboy Prince—

Except that wasn't who he was any more. The last few days he'd seemed like someone else entirely. She spun away, staring out at the unrelieved darkness of the palace gardens, the snow-covered lawns glittering in the moon-light. 'And how would your uncle take this news?'

Another hesitation. 'He'd have no choice but to accept it.'

'Really? He doesn't seem the kind of man to just…accept things.'

'No, indeed not,' Leo agreed, 'but there is little he can do with the hard fact of a marriage certificate.'

'He could make our lives miserable,' Phoebe pointed out.

'I would not allow it.' Leo took a step forward. 'And I would not allow him to bully or control Christian either—'

'*No*—' The thought of Christian being manipulated by these people made her ill. Phoebe pressed a fist to her lips. Christian was the country's *heir*. It couldn't be, couldn't be so, it was impossible, unbelievable… Something was skimming on the edge of her conscience, a realisation that she couldn't quite grasp or understand—too much had happened, too much to absorb, to accept, and yet—

And yet…

Leo was walking towards her, his stride long and sure, a look of decision in the hard planes of his face even as his eyes fastened on hers, sleepy and sensual. Phoebe took a step back, suddenly afraid. Afraid how easily she would give in if Leo touched her. She wouldn't resist at all and, while moments ago the thought had been welcome, now—now everything had changed.

'As my wife and Duchess of Larsvik you would have position, security,' Leo told her. He stood in front of her, his hands sliding along her bare shoulders, his thumbs brushing the sides of her breasts. Phoebe shuddered. She wasn't even moving or batting his hands away. 'If you don't marry me,' Leo continued, his tone so reasonable even as his hands continued to slide up and down her shoulders, skimming the curve of her breasts, making her want more, and even more still, 'where will you live? What will you do? No matter how much you try to stay in Christian's life—if you're allowed at all—you'll feel like a hanger-on. Nicholas will take every opportunity to weaken your position, your relationship with your son.'

'This can't be happening...' Yet the words came out in a moan, and she arched her body, desperate to give Leo more access. Yet he didn't deepen his caress, merely continued as he had before, his fingers skimming her body, his words no more than a breath of sound.

'But it is.'

'Your mother was married and it didn't protect her,' Phoebe gasped, and Leo's hands stilled for a moment before he resumed his caresses.

'She was a widow, young, alone, easily bullied. Your situation—our situation—is very different.'

'Is it?' She couldn't think, felt as if she could barely string two words together. Leo moved his hands to her front, his palms cupping her breasts through the thin fabric of her dress. His eyes met hers, glinting with challenge, with knowledge.

'You know it is.'

Phoebe closed her eyes, her mind spinning, her body swaying. 'I don't,' she managed, 'feel like I know anything…'

Leo reached up to lay one finger against her lips. His finger was cool and tasted slightly of salt. Phoebe realised her mouth had parted instinctively; she was practically *licking* him. 'Just say yes.'

'I…' Even in her haze of desire she hesitated, afraid, uncertain…and desperate for Leo to kiss her.

Yet Leo didn't kiss her; he simply smiled and traced the delicate line of her jaw with his thumb, the touch feather-light and yet incendiary. 'Can't you see how good it would be between us?' he murmured.

And from somewhere Phoebe found the strength to say, her voice still no more than a husky whisper, 'Sex. Just sex.'

'*Just* sex?' Leo repeated, and there was laughter in his voice, deep and rich as chocolate, and certainly just as sinful. 'You haven't had very good sex if you can say that.'

No, she hadn't. For she'd never felt like this before, as if her whole body was burning, focused on a single point, one desperate need.

Kiss me.

'You know what I mean,' Phoebe whispered. She still hadn't moved; she still stood in the circle of Leo's arms, his fingers still tracing her jaw, dropping to her collarbone, and she remembered how he'd let his finger drop lower, deeper, and she'd wanted him to…

She wanted him to now. A tiny moan escaped from her, breathless and revealing, and with a low chuckle Leo bent his head and claimed her mouth with his.

His lips were both hard and soft, Phoebe thought, cool

and warm at the same time. An exciting blend of contradictions, just like the man himself...and then she lost all track of rational thought as she was swept up into sensation, sensual pleasure, the feel of Leo's mouth moving on hers as sweet and tempting and wonderful as anything she'd ever felt or done. Even more so.

And still she wanted more. Her hands crept up to tug on the lapels of his suit, the finely cut wool sliding and catching under her grasping fingers, and with an impatient jerk she pushed the expensive fabric aside and slid her hands along his muscled shoulders, the thin cotton of his shirt the only barrier between the skin-on-skin contact she craved.

And Leo must have craved it too, for with an almost animalistic growl he lowered his head to her bare shoulder, his lips tracking kisses along her throat, and then following where his finger had gone, to the deep V between her breasts, pushing the silk of her dress aside to give himself more access to her flesh.

It was access that Phoebe eagerly, impatiently granted, and in a distant part of her pleasure-dazed mind she heard the clatter of porcelain and silver as Leo swept aside the dishes and, cradling her hips in his hands, sat her on the table.

There was something naughty and decadent about sitting on the table, her dress rucked up to her thighs, her legs wrapped around Leo's waist—when had that happened?—as if she were yet another delicious offering.

And she was an offering, Phoebe thought hazily, an offering to Leo, her body pliant beneath him, open and ready.

Her hands fisted in his hair as he moved above her, and she longed for their bodies to be joined, to feel him inside her. She *ached* with it.

And then it happened, and she gasped with surprise and

pleasure as he moved inside her, his body finally joined with hers, sliding in and fitting so perfectly, so rightly, Phoebe felt as if she'd been missing a crucial piece of herself and was finally whole.

Leo's eyes met hers as he moved; he held her gaze and neither of them looked away, needing no words. This was more than words, more necessary, more elemental.

For she'd never felt this way, this endless aching, desperate craving finally satisfied so utterly, and in the aftermath of their spent desire there emerged a new hope, a tremulous joy. This wasn't *just sex* at all. It was what she wanted, needed, and craved; it was, indeed, the purest form of communication between a man and a woman.

Leo stared at Phoebe's face, her flushed cheeks and swollen lips, framed by a wild mane of tangled curls. She looked dishevelled, beautiful and so very much his. He'd made her his.

He felt a deep, primal sense of possession as he looked at her, lying still dazed amidst the detritus of their meal. He hadn't meant it to happen like this; a bed, candles, every romantic thing he could think of waited upstairs, but he hadn't been able to get that far. From the moment he'd touched her, his mind, his sense of reason had been lost to his body's needs. And not just his body, Leo thought, for despite the urgency of their coupling he'd felt some deeper need satisfied when he'd made love to Phoebe, a final piece of himself—the most necessary piece—sliding into place.

He stood up, turning away, disturbed by the nature of his thoughts.

Slowly Phoebe slid off the table, pulling down her gown with shaky movements. Leo knew he should say something, do something besides adjust his clothes and run his hands through his hair, his movements just as shaky as Phoebe's. This was when he was meant to hold her in his arms, gain her acceptance and savour the fact that his plan had worked.

Yet he couldn't do anything.

'Leo…' Phoebe said, her voice husky.

He turned slowly to face her. 'Yes?'

She stared at him with dazed eyes, pushing her hair away from her face. 'Christian…Christian can only be named heir because he's Anders's child.'

'Of course.'

'His legitimate offspring,' Phoebe clarified, and Leo felt a well of foreboding open up inside him.

'Of course. There is no question of that. I saw your marriage certificate myself.'

'I know, but…' Phoebe licked her lips, her expression turning guarded, even fearful. Leo tensed, waiting.

'What is it, Phoebe?'

She stared at him, clearly torn between confession and self-protection. What, Leo wondered grimly, was she hiding?

'Christian…' she began, then stopped. She let out a breath and started again. 'Christian is not my son.'

CHAPTER NINE

PHOEBE couldn't read Leo's expression. She wasn't sure she wanted to. He stood there, staring at her with such ominous blankness even as her body quivered with the aftershocks of their lovemaking, the memory of his touch.

Even now she wasn't sure she should have said anything, confessed the secret she'd held so closely to her heart ever since those two government agents had shown up at her door. Yet this was the realisation that had been skimming the surface of her consciousness as Leo had begun his seductive onslaught—that, since Christian was illegitimate, he couldn't be heir.

The realisation had only fully dawned as she'd lain there, sated and dazed, after they'd made love.

Should she have told Leo? Phoebe wondered, panic starting its inevitable flutter inside her. Would he use the information against her? Yet surely not—surely not, when he'd just made love to her, asked her to marry him…

And yet, Phoebe realised dully, now there would be no reason for him to marry her. He could rescind his offer and she had absolutely no right—no reason—to feel so disappointed by the thought.

'Phoebe,' Leo finally asked, his voice so soft and yet so dangerous, 'what are you saying?'

She swallowed, knowing she would have to tell the full truth. 'He's not my son,' she repeated. 'I legally adopted him when he was three weeks old.'

Leo shook his head slowly, clearly incredulous. 'Is he *Anders's* son?'

'Yes,' Phoebe said quickly. 'Of course he is. Just look at him. You can have a paternity test done if you wish.'

Leo let out a harsh bark of laughter. 'But there's no need, if he's not legitimate.' He shook his head again. 'You'd better tell me all of it.'

'There's not much more to tell,' Phoebe said. 'Anders had an affair with a waitress in Paris before we even met. He didn't find out about the pregnancy—about Christian—until after we'd married. The girl came to him—to us—wanting to give him away.' Phoebe saw Leo's features twist with contempt. 'It wasn't like that,' she said quickly. 'If you can feel some pity for your mother, who was shamed and bullied into leaving you, then save some for this girl. She was young, only nineteen or so, and a stranger to Paris. She couldn't return home with a baby, her family would have disowned her. And she didn't have the resources to support him herself—'

'Why not ask Anders for money? Child support?'

'Perhaps she didn't know of such things. Or perhaps she knew Anders well enough not to trust him to give reliable financial support.' She sighed, remembering the fear etched in the gaunt lines of the girl's face. 'In any case, she wanted to give Christian to us, and return to her family. I was happy to take him.'

'Were you? A few weeks into your marriage?' Leo gave an incredulous laugh. 'Not much of a honeymoon.'

'No, indeed not. And I suppose that's when things

started to go sour for Anders. Married, with a child…well, it wasn't what he'd thought he was getting into.'

'So he left.'

'Yes.'

'And you kept his bastard.'

Phoebe flinched. 'You don't have to be crude,' she said. 'I'd only had Christian for a few weeks by that point, but I loved him.' She paused. 'You might as well know I was adopted myself. My biological mother was similar to Christian's—a teenaged girl without resources or support. My adoptive mother volunteered in a crisis pregnancy centre, and she encouraged my biological mother—Vanessa—to keep the pregnancy. Vanessa agreed, and my mother adopted me.' Phoebe straightened, meeting Leo's gaze. 'She was a single woman and she raised me successfully. I had a very happy, a very full childhood. So I thought I could provide the same for Christian…and I have.' Yet Christian's words from earlier that afternoon echoed through her. '*He's nice and I don't have a dad.*' She might have saved Christian from becoming king, but she'd also kept him from gaining a father.

Would Leo have made a good father, a good husband? Phoebe's heart ached. Now she would never know.

Leo raked a hand through his hair before dropping it wearily. 'Well,' he said, 'this is all very admirable.' There was a cynical edge to his voice that Phoebe hadn't heard in a while, and she didn't like it.

'I didn't tell you before because I was afraid,' she confessed quietly. 'That the king would use it as a way of taking Christian from me. But if he really is only interested in Christian as his heir…'

'Yes,' Leo agreed shortly. 'Well. I wish you'd told me this before.'

'Before,' Phoebe repeated slowly, and flushed in comprehension, and then shame. Before they'd made love. 'Why…?' She stopped, for an awful, awful realisation was starting to dawn, to creep over the horizon of her consciousness and flood her mind with damning light. 'You just made love—had sex with me to convince me to marry you,' she said. 'That's all it was.' More realisations came one on top of the other, swift and condemning. 'That's all any of it was.' She swept an arm to encompass the strewn remnants of their meal. 'This—this dinner was no more than a deliberate seduction.'

Leo's face was blank, terribly, terribly blank. He said nothing. 'And the ice-skating—the way you've been so *kind*—' She choked on the words, the thought, and spun away. Everything had been contrived, deliberately planned. None of it was real. She stared out of the window at the palace gardens, cloaked in darkness. Moonlight glinted off a bronze statue of an angel, her arms arced above her head, her face as pitilessly blank as Leo's. 'Why?' Phoebe whispered. 'Why did you do all this?'

Leo hesitated, and Phoebe spun back to face him. 'Was it just to make a fool of me? Or was it…was it some kind of revenge?'

'Of course not.' He spoke calmly, dispassionately, his face as hard as it had been that night six years ago, when he'd asked her how much money it would take to make her leave Anders.

He *was* the same man. Or he seemed like it at that moment. Phoebe closed her eyes.

'Just because something is planned,' Leo finally said, 'doesn't make it less genuine.'

Phoebe opened her eyes, stared at him in disbelief. 'You don't think so?'

'Phoebe—'

'Everything you ever did was calculated. And you told me, didn't you? "I always do my research." You probably knew pizza was Christian's favourite food, you knew—'

'Don't overreact—'

'Overreact?' Phoebe laughed shrilly. 'My entire life has been upended in the space of twenty-four hours, and the one person I was beginning to trust, to...' She stopped, not wanting to confess how deep her feelings for Leo had almost run. 'He turns out to be jerking me around.'

Leo ran a hand through his hair, exhaling in impatience. 'If it seemed like I was manipulating you, Phoebe, it was for your own sake.'

'Thanks, but I actually prefer people to be honest with me.'

'And you're one to talk of honesty!' Leo snapped. 'Keeping the truth of your son's birth to yourself! A rather important detail.'

'I was afraid—'

'Obviously you didn't trust quite so much.' Leo shook his head, his eyes now glinting with scorn. It seemed incredible to Phoebe that mere minutes before they'd been lovers. They'd looked into each other's eyes as their bodies joined and she'd felt as if she'd never known another person so perfectly, so purely. And now—

'Why do you think I tried to befriend you?' Leo demanded. He gave the answer himself, his voice hard and angry. 'So a wedding proposal from me didn't seem so *insane*.'

'You were trying to make me fall in love with you,' Phoebe whispered.

Leo laughed harshly. 'Well, it didn't work, did it?' He turned away, his hands shoved in his pockets, his body radiating anger and frustration.

Yet it had, Phoebe thought disconsolately. Or almost. She'd been on the brink of falling in love with Leo—she'd so desperately wanted to say yes to his proposal. She'd wanted to marry him—but not as a matter of convenience, but of love. The realisation levelled her, made despair flood through her in empty yet consuming waves. She shook her head now. 'It's just as well that there's no reason for us to marry, then.' As she said the words, she felt her heart twist. Amazing how quickly hope could lodge in your heart, how mere possibility could become so real—

'Actually, there is.' Leo spoke almost lazily, and Phoebe froze.

'What are you talking about?'

'We just had unprotected sex,' Leo informed her bluntly. 'I didn't wear a condom, and I'm assuming you're not using birth control.' He paused, his gaze sweeping over her, making her flush. 'Or are you?'

'No,' she admitted quietly. She hadn't any reason to use birth control, and Leo obviously had known it. He'd done his research, after all. She glanced at him, eyes flashing. 'Was that part of your plan too?'

'No,' Leo said after a moment, colour high on his cheek-bones. 'It was not. But the fact remains that it happened, and so there is a possibility you could be carrying my child.'

'A very small possibility,' Phoebe snapped.

'A real one, none the less,' Leo replied.

Her flush deepened as she realised the truth of what Leo was saying. She was in the middle of her cycle, and pregnancy *was* a possibility. She swallowed. 'Still, even if I am pregnant—'

'Your child will be my heir—'

'Not this again!' Phoebe snapped. 'The child won't be legitimate—'

'Yes,' Leo cut her off, his voice final, 'he will.' He gave her the glimmer of a smile, making Phoebe's heart lurch far more than it should. 'Or she. Queen Helena reigned for over thirty years.'

Her hand stole inadvertently, instinctively to her middle, imagining the little life nestled there. Which was ridiculous, since they'd had sex less than an hour ago. The life—the baby—they were talking about had not even been formed yet.

She looked at him curiously. 'You want this baby? That is, if this baby exists—'

'This baby,' Leo told her, 'is my heir.'

Of course. With Christian's illegitimacy, Leo was king again...which was just what he wanted.

'My news should delight you,' Phoebe said. 'With Christian out of the way, you can be king.' She smiled, as cynical as Leo had ever been. 'You should be thrilled.'

Leo paused, his face turned from hers. 'Yes,' he said tonelessly, 'of course I am.'

'But you'll have to tell the king,' Phoebe continued, a new realisation creeping over her, chilling her. 'He'll know—'

'Of course he will.'

'But who knows what he'll do? He could try to take Christian away—'

Leo gave a little snort of disbelief. 'You didn't think this through very carefully, did you?'

'Of course I didn't!' Phoebe snapped. 'I've had a dozen different things thrown at me in the last two days—I don't know what to think.' Her voice wavered and broke, and she turned away, not wanting Leo to see how overwrought she was.

'I don't think Nicholas will have much interest in

Christian once he's learned the truth of his birth,' Leo said quietly. 'He'll be of no use to him.'

'And I suppose I should be glad of that.'

'Absolutely.'

'So even though he's family, none of you want him any more,' Phoebe said dully. It should relieve her, but it still was a rejection.

'I rather thought,' Leo said after a moment, 'that it was more a case of you not wanting us.'

They were silent for a moment, the only sound the wind rattling the panes of the salon's windows and the crackle of the dying fire.

'Still,' Leo finally said, 'until we find out if you're pregnant you need to stay in Amarnes. And if it turns out you are carrying my child...' Phoebe sucked in a breath, her heart starting to hammer '...we will marry.' Leo's tone was flat, implacable. No more seduction, Phoebe thought grimly. No more pretending. Just cold, hard truth.

'I'm hardly suitable to be queen,' Phoebe pointed out. 'I wasn't before, and I haven't changed.'

Leo regarded her with assessing eyes, his head tilted to one side. 'That,' he said, 'is my decision.'

'And not mine?'

'If you are carrying my child, then no.'

It was all about the child, Phoebe thought. The heir. It wasn't about her at all. A fresh wave of realisation swept over her. It had *never* been about her. Had Leo only wished to marry her to have some control over Christian, the future king, himself? To safeguard his own interests, never mind hers?

'I'd like to go to bed,' she said in a shaky voice, and inwardly flinched as Leo's gaze flicked to the table where they'd just lain.

'Very well. We will speak tomorrow.'

Phoebe nodded, too exhausted both emotionally and physically to argue. She needed to escape the prison of this room and of her own mind—for a few hours to be blissfully blank, to think of nothing, feel nothing.

'Goodnight,' she whispered. Leo looked at her for a long moment, and she remained there, transfixed, as if he were forcibly holding her still. A darkness lingered in his eyes, a sorrow. Finally he looked away, let her go.

'Goodnight, Phoebe.'

Back in her suite of rooms, Christian settled in his own bed, she found that sleep eluded her. Phoebe lay in the middle of the king-sized bed and watched the moon cast silver shadows on the floor, her mind spinning in circles. Had she judged Leo too harshly, accusing him of being manipulative and deceitful? Perhaps he did have her best interests at heart…even if it no longer mattered. There was no reason for him to marry her, or even to be kind to her. No reason for them to have a relationship of any kind at all.

Unless she was pregnant.

Once again Phoebe's hand crept to her middle and rested there, imagining a tiny bean of a baby nestled inside her womb, starting to grow. Of course, she reminded herself, everything she and Leo had discussed was still hypothetical. *Impossible.*

Did she actually want to be pregnant? Did she want this life to grow inside her, part her, part Leo, making them a family? It would be a reason to marry Leo, even if he'd manipulated her, even if all he cared about was the crown.

I want him to be the man he's been these last few days. I want him to be real. And then, another thought that sprang unbidden from the deepest corner of her heart: *I want him to love me…as I love him.*

How could she love Leo? *Leo*…a man she'd once hated—or had that been her mind's way of protecting her heart? For even six years she'd felt that irresistible fascination with him, that dark tug of longing.

And now she loved him. She loved the man he'd shown himself to be—kind, compassionate, *passionate*… She still ached from the memory of his lips on hers, his body joined to hers…She'd never felt such pleasure, such intimacy as she had with Leo, such exquisite understanding and even joy.

Phoebe closed her eyes, desperate for sleep to come and rescue her from the endless circling of her own thoughts. She loved Leo, the Leo she'd known these last few days, and the thought that all his actions, his kind words, the way he'd *touched* her, had all been simply part of some cold-hearted plan was too awful to bear, no matter what his motive had been. She wanted him to love her, she thought despondently, and love wasn't manipulative or planned…it simply *was*.

'The king is sleeping.'

Leo gazed at the impassive face of one of Nicholas's aides and shrugged. 'Very well. I'll talk to him in the morning.'

His news about Christian could wait. Part of him wanted to gloat, to crow, to shove his victory in the old man's face. It was a childish impulse, and Leo repressed it. The information Phoebe had given him was precious, dangerous. He wasn't going to part with it so quickly.

He turned to walk down the long, dark corridor to his own room. His footsteps fell silently on the soft carpet, and all around him the palace was silent and dark.

He knew he should be feeling the thrill of victory; he'd bested Nicholas, and the old man didn't even know it yet.

He'd won the long, drawn-out battle of the last few years; he could forget all the taunts and slights, the years of being ignored, passed over, discarded. He would be king.

He wouldn't marry Phoebe.

Why did he feel so empty, so flat, so *disappointed*?

He'd enjoyed these last few days, he realised, had even come to care for Phoebe and Christian, for the family the three of them were together.

And when he and Phoebe were alone...Leo closed his eyes, sweat prickling along his shoulder blades as he remembered the touch and feel of her, all creamy skin and tangled curls...the look in her eyes, like two endless wells of longing, as he'd held her gaze and moved inside her.

He wanted that again. He wanted it forever.

Leo swore under his breath as he let himself into his private suite. The room was cast in shadow, and in the darkness he felt the old demon of guilt rise to ride him once more.

I've worked hard. I've worked so hard for it all...

He could almost hear Nicholas taunting him. *You are the aberration.*

And he was. He'd never been meant for the throne, or for Phoebe, and even now he fought the feeling—unreasonable as it might seem—that to ascend it, to marry Phoebe, would be almost a crime. The actions of a thief, who crept in quietly and took what wasn't his.

Yet if Phoebe had his child? His heir...? And he became king? Then, Leo thought grimly, he'd have everything he'd ever wanted...and he wouldn't deserve any of it.

CHAPTER TEN

THE next morning Phoebe took Christian to the nursery for breakfast. She felt an instinctive need to avoid both Leo and the king, to protect herself.

The nursery was warm and welcoming, filled with sunlight. When Frances saw them she sent for breakfast, her gaze resting on Phoebe's pale face and shadowed eyes with a little too much shrewdness.

'And how was your dinner last night?' she asked when Christian was occupied with some toy cars in the corner of the room.

'Fine,' Phoebe replied. She tried to keep her voice light but she still blushed, and Frances obviously noticed.

Desperate to change the conversation, she glanced around the room with its wide oak floorboards and comfortable furniture, the baskets of toys lining the walls. 'I'm surprised the nursery has been kept all these years. It must have been thirty years since any children were here.'

'Yes, Leo and Anders were the last ones.' Frances glanced around the room as well, and Phoebe imagined Anders and Leo there as boys, one blond, one dark. One indulged, one ignored. Baldur and Hod. Yet she suddenly found herself wondering, which was which?

She turned back to Frances. 'And have you been kept on as a governess all these years?'

Frances chuckled. 'What, twiddling my thumbs? No, indeed. I've been a nursery teacher in Njardvik. My husband was Amarnesian, and after he died I stayed on here.' She paused. 'No, I was just brought back in the last week, for this little lad.' She gestured to Christian. 'At least now the nursery will be full of laughter again. I fear it's been waiting—the whole kingdom has been waiting—for it to be used again.'

'The king hired you?' Phoebe asked, a bit too sharply, for Frances gave her a wary look.

'Not directly, of course, but yes.'

'For how long?'

Frances shrugged. 'Indefinitely. Until this little man grows up, I should think.'

Phoebe nodded slowly. It shouldn't surprise her, this news. It was no more than what Leo had told her; the king had intended to keep Christian in Amarnes. Yet still it reminded her of what Leo had known, had always known. He'd lied to her in New York, promising a two-week holiday, simply to get her to come to Amarnes. He'd kept the king's intentions from her, and then used his oh so persuasive body to convince her to marry him for his own purposes, the kingdom's purposes. To protect—and control—the heir to the throne. His throne.

It was all so obvious, so terrible, and yet Phoebe didn't want to believe it. She wanted to believe in the Leo she'd fallen in love with, yet hadn't Leo practically admitted that man was false, a charade he'd performed to win her trust?

A maid bustled in with breakfast, steaming, fragrant coffee and Danish *kringle*. Frances called to Christian, and he came over eagerly.

'Where's Leo?' he asked as he blew on his hot chocolate, a slice of *kringle* in front of him. Phoebe started in surprise.

'I don't know, scout. Does it matter?'

Christian gave her one of his looks; Phoebe had used to joke that it was the look that said he clearly knew much more than she did. 'I want to see him. He said we'd go sledging.'

'Did he?' More promises, more ways to win them over, and with a lurch of alarm Phoebe realised she needed to protect Christian's heart as well as her own. What if he became too attached to Leo? Even though their future still hung in the balance, the very real possibility remained that they would return home in less than two weeks and never see Leo again. 'I think,' she said carefully, 'that he might be busy today. Princes do work, you know.'

Christian wrinkled his nose, considering. 'Doing what?'

'Oh, lots of things…' Phoebe thought of Leo's charity for political refugees. Such generous, important work, and yet he'd been dismissive of it. *'It's easy to be admirable when you have the money and time.'*

No, she thought, it's not. Look at Anders, look at King Nicholas. Spoiled and selfish, vain and petulant. Leo was different. He *was*.

She wanted to believe it so much.

'Mom…' Christian interrupted her thoughts, his tone telling her that he'd been trying to get her attention for some minutes.

'Sorry, honey.' She smiled in apology. 'I was a million miles away.'

'Do you think we can still go sledging today?'

She glanced helplessly at Christian, who had far too

much hope in his eyes. She'd worked so hard to give him everything he needed from the moment he'd been handed into her arms, and yet now fear clutched at her heart and made her eyes sting. *I don't want you to be hurt.* 'I don't think so, Christian,' she said quietly. 'I think Prince Leopold is most likely busy today,' she told him again. With no time for them, no need to have time for them.

Christian's lip jutted out. 'I want to see him.'

'Perhaps later—'

Christian's mouth remained in a half-pout for a moment before he squared his shoulders and, nodding in acceptance, turned back to his hot chocolate. Crisis averted, Phoebe thought, but still felt a well of sadness inside her at the thought of what Christian wanted…what she hadn't even realised he'd been missing.

She reached for her coffee. 'Thank you for this,' she told Frances, who waved her hand in dismissal.

'No trouble at all.' She glanced thoughtfully at Phoebe. 'And for the lad's sake, I hope the prince is able to take you both sledging. There's meant to be snow.'

Phoebe took a sip of coffee, averting her eyes. 'I'm sure he's very busy.'

'He is, that,' Frances agreed. 'You've probably realised that Nicholas is king in name only. He's growing old, of course, and he had a stroke last year. Leo has taken on much of the day-to-day administration of the monarchy.'

Phoebe stared at the governess, her coffee cup cradled in her hands, forgotten. 'He has?' she said, and heard the blatant disbelief in her voice.

'Yes, he has. And the people love him. He has a way with them, you know, an affection and a kindness that Nicholas never had. He's like Havard, his father, that way.' She made a face before laughing a little bit. 'Nicholas hates that he can't do it all any more, of course. He's always resented Leo...but I told you that before, and you've probably seen it yourself.'

'Actually,' Phoebe said, 'I've never even met the king.' She gave a little laugh, thinking how ridiculous it was for a man she'd never met to have so much control over her life. 'I knew he resented Leo, but I didn't realise how much Leo had already taken over.'

'Nicholas still signs everything, of course,' Frances said. 'Prince Leopold is given a rather short leash, but that's just the king's way. Still, he's done so much. A new hospital in Njardvik, with a special research centre for pulmonary diseases.' Phoebe jerked in surprise, remembering Leo talking about his mother: '*She died when I was sixteen. She had a weak chest.*' 'He works for several charities,' Frances continued, 'and just recently he's authored a bill for harsher penalties for drunk-driving.' Because of Anders's death, Phoebe thought. Frances sat back complacently, her cup of coffee resting on her middle. 'Yes,' she said, 'he'll make a good king.'

Obviously Frances didn't know the king's plans regarding Christian, Phoebe thought, and was glad. She only hoped that such ignorance would continue.

They ate the rest of their breakfast in companionable silence, Phoebe lost in thought as she mulled over Frances's revelations. No wonder Leo wanted to be king, she thought. He certainly deserved it.

'Leo!' Christian's happy cry had Phoebe stiffening in her seat, afraid to turn her head, to see him and the expression in his eyes. She wondered how long he'd been standing in the doorway. How could she have not known he was there? Her body hummed and sang with awareness, and as she turned she braced herself to see him, feel his gaze on hers, cold and distant as it had been last night, when they parted.

Yet when she finally faced him, he wasn't looking cold. He was smiling, his eyes warm on hers, and Phoebe felt a ridiculous surge of relief.

'Hello, Christian,' Leo said as the boy tackled him around the knees. 'It's good to see you, too.'

Frances made herself busy cleaning up the breakfast things, and Phoebe rose from the table. 'Hello,' she said, her voice coming out a bit rusty.

'Hello.'

And then they didn't say anything, just stood there, while the memories poured through her, as warm and golden as honey, of Leo kissing her, his hands cupping her breasts, sliding down her midriff, cradling her hips.

Christian tugged on Leo's hand, and he glanced down. 'Are we going sledging?'

'Christian—'

'As a matter of fact, we are,' Leo replied easily. 'Or to-bogganing, at least.'

'What's a toboggan?'

'A very large sledge.' He glanced back at Phoebe. 'I thought we could spend a few days at the royal chalet up in the mountains.'

'Chalet?' Phoebe repeated, surprise streaking through her, even as Christian squealed in delight at the prospect.

'Yes. It's very secluded there, very private and peaceful.' He lowered his voice. 'I think it's a good idea to stay away from the palace for a little while, not to mention the Press.' He slipped a folded newspaper from his pocket and silently handed it to Phoebe.

'Oh, no.' She read the lurid headline: 'PALACE'S

MYSTERY CHILD?' There was even a blurred, grainy photo of the three of them ice-skating.

'It was bound to happen,' Leo said with a shrug. He took back the paper and put it in his pocket. 'But the less speculation, the better and, frankly, I'd rather be somewhere else.'

'Would you?' Phoebe asked in surprise. Somehow she imagined that Leo would want to be right in the centre, managing things. Yet what was there left to manage? The threat to his throne had been taken away. He could relax.

So could she, for that matter, if she didn't feel so utterly wretched.

'The chalet is only an hour from here,' he continued. 'We can drive, just the three of us. Have some proper time together.' Then, as if he'd said—revealed—too much, he added coolly, 'Unless you object?'

'No,' Phoebe said quickly. 'It sounds great.'

'Yeah,' Christian chimed in. 'Let's go!'

Leo glanced down and tousled his hair. 'My sentiments exactly.'

He was playing a dangerous game, Leo thought as he exited the nursery. He should be using the next two weeks to distance himself from Phoebe. Slowly but surely separating himself from her, from the hope she gave him, the belief that he could have it all, he could have *her.*

Yet he'd failed at the first opportunity. He'd spent several hours that morning trying to work, to keep his mind from Phoebe and the intense desire he had, in both his body and soul, to find her and drag her to the nearest bed—or table—and make love to her again. And again.

He thought he'd succeeded, had managed to get through the morning without looking for her, until he'd seen the papers. The damn newspapers, with their stories and photos and rumours and lies. And, he acknowledged starkly, too much truth. Far too much truth. The palace's mystery child, indeed.

He didn't even have a plan or thought when he'd left his study in search of Phoebe. He'd gone instinctively to the nursery, told her about the chalet, surprising himself as much as he had her. He had never intended to take her there, to have some kind of holiday, practically a *honeymoon*, even though they weren't married. Yet, if ever.

The words had been out of his mouth before he could stop them or even process his suggestion, and as Christian looked at him in delight and Phoebe in stunned silence he realised how much he wanted this. Them. A family.

A few days, he told himself now. That was all it was, all it could be. A respite for both of them, and then…

Then it would be over. Phoebe and Christian would return to New York, never to see him again. Perhaps there would be a few visits, for form's sake, as Christian was still a relation. But those would taper off eventually, and Leo would be left with nothing. He would be a stranger.

Unless she was pregnant. Leo couldn't bear to think of the possibility; it was too precarious, too precious. A child. His child. His and Phoebe's, yet if she didn't want to be married to him—if the child was a leaden chain rather than a golden cord roping them together—he shouldn't want it, surely?

Yet he did. So very much. He wanted all of it, the child, the throne, the queen.

You don't deserve it…

It didn't matter.

* * *

An hour later Phoebe and Christian waited in the quiet foyer of the palace for Leo. Christian shifted impatiently by her side.

'Where is everybody?' he asked, his voice a hushed whisper.

Phoebe shrugged. 'The king is still sleeping,' she said, 'or so I heard. I suppose you tired him out.'

'He's just tired because he's old,' Christian said with childish bluntness. 'Where's Leo?'

'I'm sure he's coming…'

'Here I am.'

'Leo!' Christian turned eagerly towards his uncle. He was coming down the stairs, dressed in jeans and a heavy parka, smiling easily.

'The Land Rover is packed and out the front, so we'd better make haste if we want to beat the snow.'

Phoebe didn't see any sign of snow as she followed Leo outside. The sky was brilliant blue, the air clear and cold. Leo took Christian from her and settled him into the car seat while Phoebe seated herself in the front. Within a few minutes they were driving out of the palace gates, through Njardvik, and then along a narrow road that snaked along the valley floor.

Phoebe didn't try to make conversation, for, despite the easy affability with which Leo addressed Christian, she saw a steeliness in his eyes, in the set of his jaw, in the way he gripped the steering wheel, that had any conversation openers dying in her throat. She had no idea what he was thinking, feeling, she realised as she turned to face the window and gaze out at Amarnes's stunning countryside.

After half an hour Leo turned onto an even narrower road that wound up the mountainside. Phoebe glimpsed a few wooden cottages and chalets among the dense evergreen trees, but other than those few buildings there was no sign of life.

They drove higher into the mountains, the rocky ground now dusted with snow, and the dazzling blue sky of that morning was now replaced with a pearly grey-white. As Leo turned the Land Rover onto a steep lane flanked by ornate iron gates, the first snowflakes began to fall.

It was perfect, Phoebe thought as they all clambered out of the car. The chalet was a rambling wooden structure with painted balconies and shutters. Perched on an out-cropping of jagged rock, it looked like something out of a fairy tale.

Their boots crunched on the snow as they walked towards the chalet, Christian racing ahead, his shouts of glee echoing around them.

Inside, the living room boasted a cathedral-like ceiling, a huge stone fireplace and a two-storey picture-window that showcased the stunning vista of both mountain and sea.

'This is amazing,' Phoebe said as Leo came in with the last of their luggage. His cheeks were reddened with cold and there were snowflakes in his hair. *He* looked amazing, Phoebe thought, swallowing.

Leo smiled. 'I'm glad you like it.'

'Are we alone here?'

'Not quite. Grete and Tobias are the caretakers when the royal family is not in residence.'

'And when they are?'

Leo shrugged. 'Normally they bring an entourage.'

'But you didn't,' Phoebe observed. Christian tugged on her sleeve, desperate to explore more of the chalet.

'I hardly think we want a bunch of dour-faced servants shadowing us,' Leo said lightly. 'Grete is probably rushing around as we speak, making sure everything is in order. I didn't give her or Tobias much warning about our arrival.'

'Actually, I was making *Julestjerner*,' a smiling, grey-haired woman said, emerging from the back of the chalet with a tray of biscuits and cups of hot chocolate, 'and Tobias is outside, making sure the sledges and skates are in order.' She turned to Phoebe, bright-eyed and unaffected. 'It's been a long time since there have been children here.' She set down the tray in front of the fireplace and turned back to Leo. 'It's good to see you, Leo.'

Leo smiled and embraced Grete with a genuine affection. 'And you too, Grete. I'm sorry there was not more warning.'

'For you, we do not need warnings.' Grete laughed.

Phoebe watched this little exchange with both surprise and curiosity. Leo spoke to this woman—a servant—with a warmth and affection she'd rarely heard, and Grete looked at Leo as she might a son. Phoebe wondered if indeed this smiling, red-cheeked woman had been a surrogate mother to Leo.

'I'm happy to meet you,' she told Grete. She glanced around ruefully. 'I'm sure my son, Christian, is around here somewhere.'

'No doubt he's found the games room downstairs,' Grete said comfortably. 'I'm sure he'll return for biscuits—children have a sense about these things!'

Indeed, Christian must have, for a few minutes later he reappeared, talking excitedly about the air-hockey table and the huge TV, not to mention the possibility of skating and sledging.

Grete's husband, Tobias, arrived, and soon they were all seated in front of the huge stone fireplace with its roaring fire, eating buttery *Julestjerner* and sipping cocoa.

Phoebe felt herself relax—fully, properly—for the first time since she'd come to Amarnes.

Christian soon went to explore the games room once more, and Grete led Phoebe upstairs to one of the bedroom suites. As she stepped into the room decorated in deep blues and greens, a fire already crackling in the hearth and the snow falling gently outside, covering the fir trees in soft whiteness, Phoebe felt herself sigh. 'This place is magical.'

Grete smiled. 'Yes,' she agreed quietly, 'it is.'

Phoebe leaned against the window frame, taking in the quiet, peaceful beauty of the trees and mountains, all covered in snow. She was glad they'd come here, she realised. It felt like a respite from the tensions and uncertainty of the palace. A very temporary one.

With Christian settled in the chalet's games room, Phoebe was alone. She tried to read a book or even to nap, but both sleep and activity eluded her. She curled up on the deep window seat and watched the snow fall and the fire snap and blaze. And missed Leo. The conversation with Grete and Tobias had shed an intriguing and welcome light on his character...on the man she wanted to believe in.

The man she *would* believe in, Phoebe thought suddenly. Wasn't love—trust—a choice? A choice she could make, to trust Leo, to trust her own faith in him. To believe in this—them—for her sake, for her child's sake. For Leo's sake.

She wanted to, she realised. She wanted it all: love, passion, happiness. She wanted it with Leo.

Yet even the thought of telling him so—opening herself, not to mention her child, to such vulnerability and pain—made her heart thump with hard, erratic beats and her palms grow damp.

She couldn't.

She couldn't risk so much…and lose. *Hurt*. Not if Leo—that Leo—wasn't real, if it really was all about manipulation, about maintaining the monarchy. Being king.

'Hello.'

Phoebe whirled from the window; Leo stood in the doorway, smiling faintly, a look of uncertainty in his eyes that made her heart beat all the harder.

'Hello. I was telling Grete how magical it is here.' Phoebe paused, sounding, feeling awkward. 'Thank you for bringing us.'

'You're welcome.' Leo strolled into the room, his hands shoved deep into his pockets. Yet, despite his casual pose, Phoebe sensed a tension from him, as if he too was aware of the awkwardness that had sprung between them.

Who are we? What can we be to one another?

She cleared her throat. 'Did you come here very much as a child?'

'Sometimes.' Leo gazed out of the window; the snow had begun to pile up in soft white drifts outside the chalet. 'As often as I could,' he added, and it sounded like a confession.

'You seem close to Grete and Tobias.'

'They are like family to me,' Leo admitted. His lips twisted briefly in a bitter smile. 'Better than family.'

We can be your family, Phoebe wanted to say. Her heart pounded in her chest. *You have me*, she wanted to add, but couldn't. She was too uncertain, too afraid, and perhaps Leo knew it, for, shaking off the mood that had sprung between them—awkward, yet intimate—he smiled wryly and gestured towards the window. 'There's plenty of snow out there. I think it's time to take Christian sledging. Will you come with us?'

Wordlessly Phoebe nodded and slipped off the window seat. At that moment, she felt as if she'd go wherever Leo wanted her to go. If only, she thought, she could tell him so.

CHAPTER ELEVEN

AFTER lunch they all trooped outside, Leo leading them to a rather steep hill piled deeply in snow. Phoebe looked at it a bit dubiously. 'That looks a little dangerous.'

'Mom!' Christian exclaimed in outrage.

'He'll be with me,' Leo told her. 'But if you think it's too much…'

Phoebe glanced at Christian, who was hopping up and down in excitement. 'No, no,' she said with a smile, 'I'm sure it will be fine.'

And it was more than fine, she soon saw; it was brilliant. Leo sat on the toboggan, Christian tucked firmly between his legs, and with one push they were shooting down the slope, Christian's shouts of joy echoing through the mountains.

Phoebe watched them trudge back up the hill, Christian's face brightly animated as he gestured to Leo, clearly reliving the highlights of the run. Leo's head was bent, snowflakes glittering in his hair and on his cheeks, smiling as he listened to Christian.

Phoebe's heart contracted. This was too much, too good, all the while knowing it wouldn't last. Couldn't. Yet for the moment she simply pushed away the knowledge that she would be leaving, that Leo would marry her only if she carried his heir and not because he loved her. For now she wanted simply to enjoy the perfection of the day, the sky as brilliant as a pearl, the dense fir trees blanketed in snow, the air so sharp and pure. And Leo. Most of all, Leo.

He smiled at her as they crested the hill. 'Your turn,' he said, a questioning lilt in his voice, and Phoebe started.

'I don't know…' She hadn't been sledging since she was a child, and even then, as a city kid, she'd only gone a few times. And that hill looked *very* steep.

'Come on, Mom,' Christian urged. 'It's *fun.*'

'I'll go with you,' Leo offered, and Phoebe imagined herself sitting snugly between Leo's thighs as he held her around the waist. She swallowed.

'All right.'

A few minutes later she was in that very position, feeling Leo's warmth against her hips and backside, his hands laced around her middle.

'Ready?' he whispered in her ear, and Phoebe's heart began to hammer in a way that had nothing to do with the snowy slope in front of her.

'Yes…'

Leo shoved off and the toboggan began to descend. 'This isn't so bad,' she began cautiously, only to let out a surprised shriek, for the toboggan had picked up speed and they were *flying.*

'Don't worry,' Leo said, his hands still holding her securely. 'I'll keep you safe.'

As the world flew by in a blur of colours, Phoebe knew he would. She leaned her head against his chest, savouring the feel of him holding her, cradling her. Keeping her safe.

All too soon it was over, and the toboggan coasted to a stop at the bottom of the hill.

'That was amazing,' Phoebe said with a little laugh as she dusted herself off. 'Really amazing.' She glanced up at Leo, who was gazing at her with an intensity that dried the breath in her lungs, the laughter on her lips.

'Phoebe…' he began, his voice low, and Phoebe's heart flipped.

'Yes,' she whispered, wanting him to say…something… *Tell me you love me. Please.*

'Come on, you guys!' Christian called from the top of the hill. 'It's my turn next!'

The moment was broken. Almost regretfully Leo shook his head and began to trudge up the hill, dragging the toboggan behind him.

That evening they shared dinner with Grete and Tobias, and, exhausted by the afternoon outside, Christian was soon bundled into bed, while Grete and Tobias had quietly withdrawn to their own quarters.

And Phoebe and Leo were left alone.

The living room was alive with leaping shadows cast by the fire's flames, and outside the world was dark and softened with snow.

'This has been wonderful,' Phoebe said quietly. She was curled up in the corner of one of the big, squashy sofas; Leo sat across from her, his legs stretched out to the fire. 'I wish I could bottle this day up and keep it forever,' she said with a little smile. 'You must have loved it here as a child.'

'I did,' Leo agreed, staring into the fire. He sounded lost in thought.

'Did you go skating and sledging?' Phoebe asked. She tried to imagine him, a dark-haired, sleepy-eyed boy with a mischievous smile. A boy who must have found his happiness here, with people who loved him.

'I spent most of my time outside,' Leo admitted with a quick, wry smile. 'There was some advantage to being the spare.'

'What do you mean?'

Leo shrugged. 'I was allowed a certain amount of freedom.' He paused. 'Anders hated it here. He was never allowed to do anything dangerous, whether it was skate or sledge or even run very fast. I sometimes wondered if that was why…' Leo stopped, his mouth tightening. He shook his head.

'Why he was so jealous of you?' Phoebe finished quietly. She remembered the look Anders had given Leo right before they'd left the palace, and she thought of the times he'd spoken of Leo, with a seemingly unwarranted bitterness.

Leo looked up, surprised. 'I suppose. I never thought…I wish he hadn't wasted his life so much,' he finally said. 'I wish I could have…' He stopped, shaking his head, memories claiming him once more.

'You weren't responsible for Anders.'

'Wasn't I?' Leo didn't give her a chance to respond to this sorrowful statement, for he shifted his position, leaning forward so the light from the fire caught the glints of amber in his hair and eyes. 'But enough of me. I want to know about you.'

'Such as?'

'You mentioned you had a very happy childhood. Tell me about it.'

Phoebe gave a little self-conscious laugh. 'Well, my mother was a potter. She still has a studio in Brooklyn. She's a bit of a bohemian, actually, and when I was growing up we always had artists and writers and poets coming through our house.' She laughed again, remembering. 'To tell you the truth, I don't think any of them were very successful. But they were passionate, at least.'

'So that's where you get it from.'

Phoebe's gaze flew to his, a blush rising. 'What do you mean?'

Leo smiled. 'Your passion…about everything.' There was no innuendo in his voice, yet Phoebe remembered all the same. Remembered the way his lips and hands had felt on her body, and how she'd craved more. She craved it now, longed to close the few feet between them and feel his body on hers once more. *I don't care if you don't love me. I just need to feel you again.*

She swallowed and looked away, not wanting Leo to see the desperate need in her eyes—not wanting him to reject her.

'You have a full life in New York now too,' Leo continued musingly. 'With your own business, friends—'

'What are you saying?' Phoebe asked, although she quickly realised she didn't want to know what he was saying. He sounded all too final, almost as if he were saying goodbye.

Leo shrugged. 'Maybe you're better off in New York…'

'No.' Leo looked at her in surprise, and Phoebe's flush intensified. 'Let's not…talk about that right now.' She took a breath, met his gaze directly. 'Let's not talk at all.'

'Phoebe…'

And then she was closing the distance between them, crossing the carpet until she was kneeling in front of him, her hands sliding along his thighs. Leo closed his eyes briefly, a muscle jerking in his jaw.

'Please, Leo, let's just…be. While we're here. This

KATE HEWITT 157

place is magical, we don't need to think about anything else. The palace or the future or anything.' She leaned forward and brushed her lips against his jaw, closing her eyes as she inhaled his scent. He smelled so good. 'Please,' she whispered.

Leo's hands came up to tangle in her hair. He turned her head so her eyes met his. 'You're sure?'

'Yes…'

'Just these few days. Just for now.'

He made it so very plain, Phoebe thought. Low expectations. *No* expectations. Well, she would take what she would get. It would have to be enough, for the thought of having nothing was too much to bear. 'Yes.'

Leo nodded, and then his lips claimed hers in a kiss so deep and drugging Phoebe swayed underneath his touch. She'd missed this. She needed this.

The only sound was the crack of the logs settling into the grate and their own ragged breathing as they moved as one, the whisper of clothes sliding to the floor and then the softer sound of skin on skin as their mouths and bodies met again and again, and the desperate craving was finally, gloriously satisfied.

It went too fast. Phoebe knew it would, knew that as soon as she and Leo silently agreed to take these days at the chalet as a time apart, a time together, they would slip by like pearls on a string, so precious and so fleeting. They spent their days with Christian, sledging and skating, building a snowman and having the inevitable snowball fight, revelling in the simplest pleasures.

One day they travelled to a nearby village, a few wooden houses and a tiny Christmas market; Phoebe couldn't resist buying one of the *nissen* on display.

And it was easy to let the cares and worries slip away in a place like this, away from the whispers and rumours, the tension and anxieties of the palace. Here there were no princes or princesses, dukes or duchesses, no heirs at all. They were simply a family, mother, father, son.

Husband, wife. Or as good as. For, while the days were filled with fun, the nights held an even deeper joy as Phoebe learned Leo's body and he hers. Under the cover of darkness, they needed no words beyond a few provocative murmurs: *Do you like this? What about that?* The low, shared laughter of lovers, and the dazzling wonder of shared pleasure, deep and intense.

As she lay in Leo's arms it made Phoebe's heart ache to think it might end. Yet perhaps it wouldn't end. She found herself imagining the child she might be carrying, with her eyes and Leo's hair and smile. She pictured it nestled inside her, protected, cherished…for she wanted this baby, wanted it desperately. She wanted it for itself, a tiny, perfect life, but also as a reason to stay, a reason for Leo to marry her. Perhaps he didn't love her now, perhaps he saw her as only a means to an end, but the last week had shown her he had affection for her, and certainly attraction. Couldn't both grow into love? Could she will Leo into loving her, she wondered, for surely if she could, he would? She'd never wanted anything so much.

Inevitably it all came to an end. The few days they had planned to be away had been extended, and now it had been ten days since she and Leo had first made love; even though he hadn't said anything, Phoebe knew they would soon be returning to the palace, to reality. She would explain to Christian, who had accepted this new life with such amazing ease, that they were going back to New York. Home…except right now it didn't feel like home. This—Leo—did.

That night Phoebe lay next to Leo, one hand resting on his chest, the sheets tangled about their naked bodies. The only light in the room came from the fireplace, where a few orange embers still burned. Outside the world was hushed and expectant; Leo had told her it was meant to snow again.

'I wish we could spend Christmas here,' Phoebe said. The holiday was still over a fortnight away, and by that time Phoebe knew she would most likely be back in New York. Still, she couldn't keep from voicing her wish.

'There are royal duties at Christmas time,' Leo said, and left it at that. His royal duties, Phoebe supposed, not hers. Her hand crept to her middle once more. Unless…

'However,' Leo continued, a slight, surprising note of hesitation in his voice, 'I do have a present for you.'

'You do?' Phoebe heard the blatant surprise in her voice, and obviously Leo heard it too, for he chuckled.

'Is that so shocking? I bought it at the Christmas market in the village.' Leo rolled out of bed and went to the bureau, taking a paper-wrapped package from it. 'It is a small thing, but I thought you might like it.'

'I'm sure I will,' Phoebe whispered as Leo handed it to her. It was a small box, she could tell, with a satisfyingly heavy weight.

'Open it,' he urged when Phoebe remained still, gazing down at the wrapped box. 'That's what you do with presents, you know.'

'I know.' Phoebe smiled, although she felt strangely emotional. Was this a farewell present? she wondered. Slowly she undid the wrapping and opened the box. A necklace nestled inside, a perfect teardrop topaz on a slender gold chain. Phoebe lifted it to the light, which caught the topaz and turned it to fire. 'It's beautiful,' she whispered. 'Thank you.'

Leo shrugged. 'It's a trifle, nothing like any of the crown jewels, but…' He hesitated, and Phoebe, in the act of fastening it around her neck, looked up. 'I thought it would look nice on you,' he finished. 'To bring out the gold in your eyes.'

'My eyes are grey,' Phoebe protested. Leo moved around the side of the bed to fasten the clasp, his fingers lingering on her skin.

'Grey with gold flecks,' he corrected. 'You can only see them up close.' His breath feathered her cheek and, even though they had made love only moments ago, Phoebe found herself weak and dizzy with desire once more. She leaned back against Leo and, the necklace now clasped, he reached around her to cup her breasts in his palms, drawing her closer to him.

They remained that way for a moment, silent, not needing words. The only sound in the room was the hiss and crackle of the dying fire and their own quiet breathing.

Leo bent to kiss her neck, his hands sliding down her navel, fingers teasing, and Phoebe shuddered in response. He knew just how to touch her, knew exactly what made her crazy with need.

And she knew too. She turned around, sliding her legs around his hips, smiling a little as she heard his indrawn breath when she drew him inside her.

They moved slowly, in an exquisite rhythm, never speaking, never taking their eyes off one another, even as the pleasure intensified and Phoebe cried out, their bodies coming together and climaxing as one.

She'd never felt so close to another person, and yet there had been a finality about their lovemaking that made her heart ache. Please, she thought, don't let this be goodbye.

'I have a present for you too,' she said afterwards, as they lay on the bed once more, their limbs tangled so she didn't know where she ended and Leo began.

'You do?' Leo sounded so surprised Phoebe couldn't help but smile.

'It really is a trifle. But...' Suddenly she felt shy, even vulnerable. 'I thought of you when I saw it,' she said, and went to fetch her own package from her handbag by the bureau.

'What could it be?' Leo murmured as he took it, unwrapping the tissue paper. Phoebe nibbled her lip nervously as he undid the paper, staring down at the little hand-carved *nisse*.

'I liked him,' she said after a moment when Leo didn't speak, 'because he looked a bit friendlier than some of the others. Like he wouldn't play tricks on you.' Then, driven by a need she could not name, she reached down and wound a stray lock of Leo's hair around her finger, her thumb caressing his cheek. 'So you must have been a good boy.'

Still Leo didn't speak, and Phoebe wondered if she'd made a mistake. When she'd seen the *nisse* at the Christmas market yesterday, she'd thought of Leo's sorry childhood and wanted to buy it for him. Yet now it seemed wrong somehow, as if she'd been trying to heal a huge wound by offering a sticking plaster.

Finally Leo looked up, his throat working, his eyes suspiciously bright. 'Thank you,' he said, and his voice sounded hoarse. 'It's a wonderful present.'

If she'd had any doubt about whether she loved him—whether he was someone she should love—it fell away in light of the fierce joy of Leo's expression. Suddenly all her doubts and fears seemed ridiculous, irrelevant. Suddenly she was sure.

Leo was that man…the man underneath, the man she'd hoped he was. It was so obvious, had been made apparent in a thousand little ways, from the way he played with Christian, to how he helped Tobias carry in the wood, to the way he'd held her gaze with such certainty as they'd made love.

And she wanted to tell him. She would tell him. Phoebe dropped to her knees, her hands reaching up to cradle his face. 'Leo…'

He stood up, slipping away from her like quicksilver. 'It's late, and we should sleep. Tomorrow we must return to the palace.'

Phoebe dropped her arms, empty and aching. Leo couldn't have been plainer; he didn't want to hear declarations of love from her. He simply wanted to return to the palace. 'All right,' she said dully.

Leo moved to the cupboard and opened a drawer, then handed Phoebe a slim white box. 'I picked this up in the village. You can take it tomorrow morning.'

Phoebe stared down at the pregnancy test. 'It hasn't been two weeks—'

'Apparently you can take them earlier these days,' Leo replied. 'And it's better to know sooner.' His voice was flat, final. Phoebe's fingers curled around the box.

'All right,' she said again, for the fight—the hope—had gone out of her. The magic had ended.

She woke early the next morning, with Leo still asleep beside her, and slipped into the bathroom. She stared at the box with its blazing script: *Test five days early! 99.9% accurate results!*

'What if I don't want to test early?' she muttered. She'd thought she had five more days. Five more days of loving Leo, being with him…

But no. The balance of her life was in this box, and suddenly Phoebe realised she actually wanted to know. Wouldn't it be better to know, to be able to move on with her life sooner, if that was the case?

And if she was pregnant…to begin to build her life with Leo.

She ripped the plastic off the box, her heart thumping. She read the rather simple instructions several times, just to be sure, and then she took the test.

The ensuing three-minute wait was agonising. Phoebe turned the stick over so she wouldn't be tempted to look. She'd brought a watch into the bathroom, and she kept her gaze on the second hand as it moved with tiny ticks around the watch's face. She heard Leo stir in the bedroom, and then knock on the bathroom door.

'Phoebe…?'

'Just a minute,' she called. Literally.

Leo was silent, and Phoebe knew he was also waiting. Waiting for the result, for their future…if they had one.

The three minutes were up. Her heart beating so fast her vision swam, Phoebe picked up the stick and turned it over. She stared at the blazing pink line.

One line. She wasn't pregnant.

'Phoebe?' Leo's voice was low yet insistent on the other side of the door. 'Are you taking the test?'

'Yes…' Desperately Phoebe scrabbled for the instructions in the box: 'One line… One line means you're not pregnant. If you don't get your period, try again in three days.'

Three days! She had three more days at least, just to be sure. The test was early, after all…

'Phoebe,' Leo called again. 'Open the door.'

'All right.' She felt numb, lifeless. Only then did she

realise how much she'd been holding on to that dream, the hope she was pregnant. Now there was no reason to stay, no reason at all.

'Well?' Leo demanded when she opened the door. He searched her face, as if he could find clues in her frozen expression.

'I'm…' Phoebe stopped, started again, her voice toneless despite the misery swamping her heart. 'I'm not pregnant.'

'Not…' Leo repeated in a hiss of breath. His eyes met hers. 'Not,' he said again, and she thought she heard sorrow, regret. 'Well, that's good, then. For the best,' he clarified.

'Yes,' Phoebe managed to say. She couldn't bring herself to tell him about the three-day wait, the possibility of a false negative. Suddenly it didn't matter.

'Not pregnant,' Leo repeated, and Phoebe wondered if he'd been imagining their baby—the reality of their baby—too. He sounded shocked. 'Well.'

'Well. So this is it.' There was nothing more to say, Phoebe thought, yet still they both stood there, staring at each other, wanting…

At least, she wanted. Wanted Leo to take her in his arms, to tell her he loved her as she loved him, that there would be other babies, other opportunities for babies, that they could have a lifetime of living and loving together. She felt the words on her tongue, opened her mouth to let them spill out, when Leo spoke first.

'Phoebe.' She stared at him eagerly, hungrily, waiting. 'Yes…'

Leo gazed at her, his eyes intent on hers, and Phoebe felt the moment stretch and open up between them. Surely, she thought, surely he loves me. Surely he'll tell me now…

Leo opened his mouth, but whatever words he'd been going to speak were drowned by the tinny trill of his mobile phone, his direct line to the palace, and from the sudden blanking of his expression Phoebe knew the moment had passed. She prayed it wasn't gone for ever.

Leo turned away from her and reached for the mobile. He spoke tersely into the phone; Phoebe couldn't understand the rapid-fire Danish. Yet when he turned back to her his expression was so bleak she knew something terrible had happened.

'It is the king,' he told her.

'The king,' Phoebe repeated numbly, and Leo nodded.

'King Nicholas is dead.'

CHAPTER TWELVE

EVERYTHING had changed. It happened so quickly; one minute she and Leo had been in their bedroom, on the precipice of—what? A declaration of love? Phoebe had thought so, had prayed so. She'd almost said those three amazing, life-changing words, *I love you*. And she'd begun to believe that Leo might say them back.

Then, in the next minute, their entire world, as new and fragile and barely there as it was, had been irrevocably changed. Damaged, or perhaps even destroyed…if it had ever existed in the first place. Within minutes of the phone call from the palace, Leo was motivating the household, packing his bags and asking Tobias to bring the car round.

'But Leo,' Phoebe protested, throwing clothes on with haphazard haste, 'it's six o'clock in the morning. Christian—'

'Will adjust,' Leo finished. He wasn't even looking at her, Phoebe saw. He dressed with clinical haste, his expression distant and hard. Thinking of the palace, Phoebe thought. Of himself as king. After the last few days, he was reverting to the old Leo—the Leo she'd hoped wasn't real, true—like a snake sliding into its true skin.

Phoebe had woken Christian, saying only that an emergency back at the palace required them to leave at once.

'What's happened?' Christian asked, blinking sleep from his eyes even as they became shadowed with worry. 'What's wrong?'

Everything, Phoebe wanted to answer. 'It's the king,' she told Christian quietly.

'What happened?'

Phoebe shook her head. 'I don't know what happened exactly,' she prevaricated, not wanting to break the news to Christian without knowing more details. 'We'll find out when we return.'

They drove in silence along the narrow, twisting roads, the world cloaked in snowy darkness. Phoebe sneaked glances at Leo and saw that his hands were clenched tightly around the steering wheel, his knuckles white. She wondered what he was thinking. Feeling. No matter how fraught or damaged the relationship between Leo and Nicholas had been, he was still his uncle, and Leo had lost two close relatives in a matter of weeks.

Phoebe leaned her head back against the seat and closed her eyes. She felt a wave of fatigue—emotional, physical—crash over her. She couldn't bear to think any more. To wonder. She wanted answers. She wanted honesty. Yet she could hardly demand such things from Leo now, when his mind was taken up with matters of state.

Yet still her mind and heart cried out, *Do you love me?* Had he been about to tell her so?

Servants waited outside the palace as Leo drove up in the Land Rover. As soon as he'd parked the vehicle he was out of the door, conferring in hurried, hushed tones with several important-looking officials. Phoebe was left to deal with Christian, and when she turned around again Leo was gone.

She didn't see him again that day. She spent the day in the nursery with Christian, playing with tin soldiers—had they been Leo's once?—and trying not to think. Yet still her mind spun in hopeless circles. What had Leo been going to say? What would he have said if she'd had enough courage to tell him she loved him? *What was happening?*

Frances was tight-lipped for once too, and several times she glanced out of the long, wide windows to the court-yard below, the flag lowered and the gates draped with black crêpe, as if news could be had there.

After an early supper with Frances and Christian, Phoebe settled Christian in bed and then stretched out on a sofa in her suite's little parlour, too tired and dispirited to do anything more.

She should make plans to return to New York, she realised. Arrange plane tickets, pack her bags. They could leave tomorrow, even. There was no reason to stay; Leo had made that abundantly clear by his absence. From the moment he'd returned to the palace he'd been concerned with matters of state, and it was as if she and Christian no longer existed. To all intents and purposes, they didn't.

Phoebe closed her eyes, fighting another wave of sorrow. It was better this way; Leo had shown his true colours. A marriage for convenience's sake would have been miserable, soulless. The life she'd been quietly weaving for herself—a husband, a baby, a family—was no more than a dream or a mirage. False. Non-existent.

Yet even as these thoughts circled sluggishly in her brain, Phoebe knew she could not just lie there and wait for life to happen...or not happen, as the case may be. She would find Leo. She would confront him. She would demand the truth, as cold and hard as it undoubtedly was, and then she would go home.

She rose from the sofa, straightening her hair and clothes before she headed out into the shadowy corridors of the palace in search of Leo.

Leo took off his glasses and rubbed his eyes. He ached with tiredness. He'd been in meeting after meeting that day, with Parliament, with palace staff, with the Press. Always seeking to undo the damage Nicholas's last days had caused, stabilising the monarchy.

His monarchy. He was king. He rose from the desk and moved to the window, gazing out at the palace courtyard now strung with lights. In their eerie glow he could see the lowered flag, the draped crêpe. The king was dead; long live King Leopold.

He turned back to the desk, his heart twisting within him. This was what he'd always wanted, from the moment perhaps when he knew he'd never have it. Yet why, then, was he so unhappy, so empty?

I don't deserve it…

He silenced the voice of his conscience; it didn't matter if he deserved it or not. He was king, he would strive to be a good one, to serve his country and his people with his whole heart.

His country would have his heart, for no one else could claim it. Where was Phoebe? he wondered. Had she gone already, slipped from the palace like a shadow? There would be no need to say goodbye. The time they'd enjoyed at the chalet had been an idyll, separate and finite. And now it was over. She'd made that clear when she'd told him she wasn't pregnant. '*So this is it.*' He'd almost—almost— told her he loved her, begged her to stay even if she didn't love him, even if there was no reason. He was glad he hadn't had the chance, for surely Phoebe was better off in

New York, living her full, happy life without the intrigues of the palace, without him.

The door to the study creaked, and Leo looked up in surprise. In the slice of light made by its opening he saw a head of curly hair, the flash of a wide grey eye. Phoebe. His heart lurched in his chest and he straightened, laying his palms flat on the table, knowing what he must do.

'Come in, Phoebe.'

He spoke so flatly, Phoebe thought, so impersonally, as if she was simply one more person—one more problem— to deal with. She slipped into the room, her gaze taking in the scattered papers on Leo's desk, half a dozen newspapers with their blazing headlines: *The King Is Dead. King Leopold Ascends the Throne.*

'Congratulations,' she said, her voice scratchy. Was that what you said to a king? She had no idea.

Leo inclined his head in acknowledgement. 'I will try my best to be a good king to the people of Amarnes.' His voice was still flat.

'Yes. I know you will.' Phoebe's throat ached with the effort of not crying. She wanted to cry, to let all the sorrow and disappointment out, to demand of Leo, *What was last week, then? Did you never love me at all?* She swallowed it back down; surely she didn't need him to spell it out for her, hear his cold rejection of her face to face? She tried to smile and didn't quite manage it. 'So...I thought I should probably book my plane tickets back to New York. Josie, my assistant, must be going crazy.'

'Right.' Leo slipped on a pair of glasses, and the little gesture made Phoebe's heart ache. She didn't know he wore glasses; how many little things did she not know about him? Now she would never find out. 'You can fly back on the royal jet,' he told her. 'It's the least I can do.'

'Thanks.' She swallowed. 'That's very generous of you.'

'It's nothing.'

And, Phoebe thought, considering all they'd shared, it felt like nothing. She stood there, feeling surplus to requirements and slightly ridiculous, but she couldn't bear to go, to end it like this.

'Christian is still your nephew,' she blurted. 'Will you...will you want to see him?'

Leo gazed at her quietly for a moment. 'Do you want me to?'

Phoebe felt a sudden spurt of rage at his obvious indifference. 'You've managed to matter to him these last two weeks,' she said, her voice cold. If she stayed angry, she wouldn't cry. She wouldn't hang on to Leo's sleeve and shame herself by begging him to let her stay.

'He matters to me,' Leo said quietly, so quietly Phoebe almost didn't hear him.

'Does he, Leo?' she asked, and heard the stinging scepticism in her own voice. 'Does he really?'

Leo jerked his head upwards, his eyes flashing. 'Of course he does, Phoebe—'

'Because,' Phoebe cut across him, 'it doesn't seem like it from here. From here it seems like you were just using him the way you were using me.'

Leo's eyes widened, then narrowed, the corners of his mouth turning white. 'Using him?' he repeated dangerously. 'How was I using him, Phoebe?'

'To stabilise the monarchy,' Phoebe retorted, throwing his own words back at him with a bitter, sarcastic edge. 'And the only way to do that is to sit on the throne yourself, right? Except if Christian was named heir, you couldn't, so the next best thing was to be the heir's guardian. Were you hoping to become regent? Control him that way? And then I gave you the best news of all—you could be king!' Tears started at the corners of her eyes, and she bit her lip hard to keep them from sliding down her cold cheeks. 'Only I told you a little too late, and poor you, you had to sleep with me first—'

'Phoebe—'

'What an *inconvenience*,' Phoebe cut him off, one tear escaping to trickle down her cheek.

'Where,' Leo asked in a low voice, 'are you getting these ideas?'

'From you,' Phoebe cried. 'What am I supposed to think, Leo, when you rush us back to the palace at the crack of dawn and then deposit us on the front steps like so much unwanted rubbish? And not a single word all day—nothing! And you know why?'

Leo's eyes glinted with silent menace, his lips compressed in a hard line. 'No,' he said, his voice cold and clipped. 'Why?'

'Because we don't matter to you any more,' Phoebe threw at him. 'Christian is illegitimate and I'm not pregnant, so you're done with us! Isn't that right?' She planted her hands on her hips, giving him a glare of angry defiance even as her heart begged, *Please tell me how wrong I am. Please tell me all these fears are groundless. Don't let me walk out of here...*

'Well.' Leo glanced down at his desk and mindlessly straightened some papers. When he looked up again, his expression was entirely too bland. 'You seem to have worked it all out.'

Phoebe's chest hurt with the effort of keeping all the

emotion inside. Was that all he was going to say? Not one word of explanation or apology? Obviously he had none to give. She drew in a shuddering breath. 'I suppose I have.'

They stared at each other for a long, aching moment; Phoebe felt all the pain and sorrow—the disappointed, destroyed hope—rise up within her, threatening to come out in a howl of misery. She felt it in every aching part of her body, knew it was reflected in her tear-filled eyes. Leo, however, merely looked bland. His eyes and mouth possessed a certain steeliness, making Phoebe wonder if she'd actually *annoyed* him. Nothing more. Finally she spoke.

'I should go.'

Leo's only response was an indifferent jerk of his shoulder; his eyes remained cold. With leaden heart and feet, Phoebe slowly turned around. She walked to the door, hardly able to believe this was goodbye. For ever. After everything—the days and nights they'd shared, the caresses, the whispers and secrets—he was letting her walk out of his life without even saying goodbye. She choked back a cry at the thought, steeling her spine, and put her hand on the knob. Then Leo spoke.

'The reason I was closeted all day with government officials,' he said in a strange, scratchy voice that wasn't like his at all, 'was to keep a coup from taking place.'

Phoebe's hand curled around the doorknob, her back still to Leo. 'A coup?' she repeated in disbelief.

'Yes. You see, no one knew about Christian's birth.'

She turned around slowly. Leo was staring at her with blazing eyes, his face white. Phoebe couldn't tell if he was angry or possessed by some other, deeper emotion. Hurt. 'Why didn't they know?' she whispered. 'Didn't you tell Nicholas?'

Leo hesitated for a fraction of a second. 'No, I didn't,' he said quietly. 'I knew he was dying. It was only a matter of days, maybe weeks. It occurred to me that if he did know, he could make life...unpleasant. For you and Christian.'

Phoebe's heart lurched. 'You mean sue for custody?'

'Something like that. Nicholas is—was—like an old bear, grouchy and mean. He was perfectly capable of making someone's life a misery simply because he could.'

'So when you returned—'

'Nicholas had changed his will,' Leo said, 'and he had enough cronies who would bid for power through Christian if he were king. I had to show Parliament that Christian was ineligible. We had his birth certificate faxed from Paris. His mother was Leonie Toussaint. A waitress like you said, only nineteen years old.' He shook his head. 'Poor girl.'

'Yes,' Phoebe whispered. 'You could have told me—'

'I didn't want you or Christian brought into the limelight,' Leo replied. 'In any case, we handled it with quick discretion, and the stories in the papers will soon be squashed.'

'And you'll be king,' Phoebe finished dully. 'Congratulations. You have everything you've ever wanted.'

Something flashed across Leo's face, streaking through his eyes and tightening his muscles, and when he spoke his voice was terse and strangled. 'Do you think,' he asked, 'that I did all this simply so I could be king?'

Phoebe stared. 'What else should I think?'

Leo gave a short, harsh laugh and turned away. 'I never thought I deserved the throne, Phoebe, and it appears you agreed with me.'

Phoebe's mind whirled with the implications of his

words. 'What are you saying, Leo? Of course you deserve the throne. You're next in line in the succession—'

'An accident of birth does not mean anything,' Leo cut her off. 'You should know that. Look at Anders. He was dismally prepared to be king, so much so that he escaped it the first opportunity he could.'

'So why do you think you don't deserve to be king?' Phoebe asked, and Leo turned back to face her.

'Why do you think I want to be king so much, Phoebe?' Leo returned softly.

'Because…' she shook her head, feeling as if Leo had taken the chessboard of their conversation and scattered all the pieces '…because everything you did was for that. Taking me to Amarnes, asking to marry me—'

'Was to gain control of Christian rather than protect the two of you, keep you from being manipulated, trampled on like my mother was?' Leo filled in. 'What kind of man do you think I am, Phoebe?'

Phoebe flushed. Suddenly her words, so carelessly and angrily spoken, seemed hurtful. Callous, and perhaps even wrong. 'I thought you were a good man,' she whispered. 'When we were at the chalet, and even before…you seemed such a kind man.'

'*Seemed?*' The word was a sneer.

'Yes.' She took a breath, willing herself to continue. Now was the time for total honesty, her last chance, when there surely was nothing left to lose. 'You seemed,' she continued, 'like a man I could fall in love with.' Leo gave a little laugh of disbelief, and Phoebe realised how weak her words sounded. 'I did fall in love with you,' she clarified, her cheeks flushing. 'And I hoped you'd fallen in love with me.'

'So what made you change your mind?'

'What do you mean?'

'Come on, Phoebe.' Leo gestured to the door, still half-open. 'You were about to walk out of here. You came to find me to tell me you needed to buy plane tickets. The truth is, you couldn't wait to leave.'

'No, Leo,' Phoebe returned, shaken, 'that's not true at all—'

'And I don't blame you,' Leo continued savagely, riding over her words, not hearing them. His eyes glittered with pain and anger. 'The only reason I didn't keep you here— get down on my knees and beg you to stay—is that I know how much better off you'd be in New York.'

'What?' Phoebe stared at him in shock and disbelief even as hope was starting to turn crazy somersaults all through her body, making her dizzy. She reached out one steadying hand to his desk. 'Leo—what on earth makes you say that? Think that?'

'I don't deserve you, Phoebe,' Leo said bleakly. He swept an arm to encompass the royal study, the palace, perhaps his entire kingdom. 'I don't deserve any of this.' Phoebe heard a well of despair deep in Leo's voice, a despair that she sensed had been plumbed long, long ago, when he'd been told and shown in a thousand little ways how unneeded he was. How undeserving. And obviously he believed it.

'Leo, *deserving* anything never came into it for me—'

'Well, it should have—'

'Does anyone deserve love?' Phoebe pressed. 'Love simply is. And I love you—'

'You don't know me,' he said in a low voice. He averted his head once more, his face in profile. 'You don't know what kind of man I am, what I'm capable of.'

Phoebe had thought the same thing once, back when

Leo had scared and intimidated her. When she hadn't known what kind of man he was…but she'd found out. She'd discovered it for herself when she'd lain in his arms, when she'd seen him smile at Christian, in so many small ways and instances, treasured memories locked in her heart. She *knew* Leo.

'I think I've come to know you,' she said carefully, 'in the last two weeks—'

'*Weeks,*' Leo dismissed in contempt. 'And if you knew me so well, Phoebe, how could you come down here and accuse me of all the things you did? How could you believe I'd marry you simply to control Christian, make him some kind of puppet ruler?'

Phoebe flushed in shame once more. 'I was angry, and I wanted to make you say something—deny it—'

'And I will deny it,' Leo returned with some heat. 'I intended to marry you to protect you, Phoebe, from Nicholas's machinations, and the machinations of his cronies at court. Even after he was dead…without a protector, Christian would have been vulnerable. Trust me,' he smiled bleakly, 'a boy alone at court is not an easy thing.'

Phoebe's heart ached. 'No,' she whispered, 'I'm sure it's not.'

'But not to control or manipulate him, I swear.' He held up a hand to forestall her argument, even though Phoebe had none. 'I know you believe I manipulated you in trying to get you to marry me. And that is true, in a way. I was kind to you with—with a goal in sight, but also because I wanted to marry you. I wanted to be with you.' He paused, and when he spoke again his voice was ragged. 'I even wanted our child.'

'So did I,' Phoebe admitted with a shaky laugh, and Leo smiled sadly.

'If only…' Why, Phoebe wondered, did he sound so regretful? So final? As if, even now, they couldn't be together?

'Leo…'

'There are other things…' He stopped, shaking his head.

And Phoebe cried, 'What other things, Leo? What do you feel so…so *guilty* about?' He pressed his lips together, saying nothing, and Phoebe continued hesitantly, 'Is it the way you lived before…the women, the parties? The wild lifestyle?' His years as the Playboy Prince. Did he feel so guilty about that after all this time? Leo didn't reply, and Phoebe forced herself to continue. 'Because it was a long time ago and since then—'

Leo gave an abrupt, harsh bark of laughter. 'Do you think this is about a few parties? Or even a few women? Do you think I'm torturing myself over a little wild living?' He sounded so sneeringly incredulous that Phoebe flushed.

'I don't know,' she admitted. 'What is it about, Leo?'

'You want the truth, Phoebe?' he finally said. It wasn't a question; it was a reckoning. 'You want to know what kind of man I am? Then you won't delude yourself into thinking you love me, thinking we could have had anything more than a convenient marriage—than just sex!' His voice rang out, and Phoebe flinched. 'This is the kind of man I am,' Leo said raggedly. He sounded as if he'd been running, as if he was now gasping for air, for life. 'I hated Anders. I always hated him. It wasn't just petty jealousy, some kind of sibling-type rivalry. No,' he said, giving her that terrible smile she remembered from before, 'it's more than that, worse than that. I hated him for all I had to do for him, and all he never did. For all he had and threw away…even you. Especially you.'

'Leo—'

'I hated him so much I was *glad* when he abdicated. I wanted him to walk away. I didn't try very hard to keep him there, did I? Do you remember?' He turned around, took a dangerous step towards her, his eyes glittering. 'There's more than one way to buy someone off, isn't there, Phoebe? You might not have taken money ten years ago, but you would have taken me.' Then, as if he hadn't made it damningly clear enough, he continued, 'I could have seduced you, Phoebe. It would have been all too easy. I could have made you leave him.'

'Then why didn't you?' Phoebe challenged, her face hot with memory and shame.

'Because I wanted Anders to leave.' His voice was a sneer of self-loathing. 'I thought—maybe then—I'd be free. Free of him. But of course I wasn't. I might have been heir, but Nicholas never forgot who was meant to be king. And neither did I.' He turned away, tension and anger—directed, no doubt, at himself—radiating from every taut line of his body. 'So that's the kind of man I am. A man who's been consumed by hatred for far too long, there's no longer any room for love.' He spoke in a flat, final voice that shook Phoebe to the very core.

'Hatred,' she finally said, 'or guilt?'

Leo shrugged. 'It hardly matters.'

'Doesn't it?' Phoebe challenged quietly. She looked at him now, a man in the grips of a horrible memory, an agony of guilt. Guilt, not hatred. At that moment she wondered if Leo had hated Anders at all. She thought of the harsher laws for drunk-driving, the centre for pulmonary diseases. She'd thought they'd been merely the actions of a good king, but Phoebe saw now they'd been something else as well. Atonement. Atonement for a past

Leo had been unable to control, for being the older son but the younger cousin. For wanting to be responsible, and unable to be it…be anything. 'You weren't responsible for Anders, Leo—'

'I was *older*—'

'So?'

'It was my duty—'

'Is that what they told you?' Phoebe guessed. 'You were the one meant to keep Anders's nose clean? And,' she finished, realisation and memory sweeping through her, 'to clean up his messes.' As she had been six years ago…and even two weeks ago. She'd been Leo's job, just another mess to clean up.

'Someone needed to,' Leo said, and Phoebe shook her head.

'Perhaps everyone believed that, but Anders, like anyone else, had to be responsible for his own life. His own mistakes. And he chose his own path, all the way to the end.'

'I never stopped him,' Leo confessed raggedly. 'I should have, God knows I should have, but I never did.'

'You mean,' Phoebe guessed quietly, 'you were never able to stop him.'

Leo shrugged. 'It amounts to the same.'

'I don't think it does.' Phoebe met his gaze directly. Despite the despair in Leo's eyes she felt hope; it coursed through her veins like liquid gold, shining and pure. 'I don't blame you, Leo,' she said. She kept her voice calm and steady, even though it took so much effort. She felt as if she might splinter apart, body and soul, into a thousand agonised fragments of fear. To lose him now—to this! To the past, which was finished, a sorrowful chapter that had ended long ago, even if it had kept Leo in its tortured pages. 'If I were you, I would hate Anders too. And I don't think you hated him as much as you hated what he did, the man he became. The waste he made of his life, when he'd been given so much.'

'I should have helped him,' Leo said after a moment. 'I could have—'

'How? Who would have let you? Not Anders.' She took a breath. 'I think perhaps Anders resented and even hated you.' She felt a jagged shard of sorrow lodge in her soul at the thought of so much bitterness. Baldur and Hod, indeed.

'He did hate me,' Leo said in a low voice, 'because he knew I hated him.'

'Or maybe,' Phoebe countered, 'he hated you because neither of you were ever given the chance to love each other. You were forced into impossible roles as little boys, and there was never any chance for a normal kind of relationship.'

'That's true,' Leo acknowledged after a moment, 'but it doesn't change—'

'The kind of man you are? I *know* what kind of man you are, Leo.' Leo shook his head, an instinctive movement, refusing to accept the hope Phoebe offered. The love. But she wasn't done yet, not by a long shot. She took a step closer to him, even though everything in him was telling her to stay away…everything but the look of hungry desperation in his eyes. 'You know what I think, Leo?' Phoebe asked softly. 'I think everything you've told me makes you a better man, not a worse one. You hated the waste Anders made of his life, and yet you still made a sacrifice of yours.'

'Only because—'

'It doesn't matter *why*,' Phoebe cut him off. 'It doesn't even matter what you thought. Only what you *did*, Leo, for your cousin, for your king. For your mother too. Actions are what count. Love is a verb, after all, isn't it?

And I love you, not just in what I say, but also in what I do. I believe in you. I think you'll make a wonderful king. And…' she took a breath, laying it all out there, needing to, *wanting* to '…and a wonderful husband. And father. If I ever get the chance to know—'

'Oh, Phoebe…' Leo shook his head, his voice breaking.

'Love is an action,' Phoebe continued steadily, 'and it's also a choice. I choose to love you. All of you, all the mess and mistakes and regrets, and all the wonderful parts too.' She was close enough now to touch him, so she did, reaching up to slide her hands along his shoulders and then up to cup his face. 'I love the man you are with my child. I love that you thought about his needs, even when no one asked you to, when no one was looking. I love the way your eyes gleam with laughter when you talk to him…and I love the way you look at me when we're making love. Love,' she emphasised, drawing him closer—so thankful he didn't resist. 'I love you.'

Leo rested his forehead against hers, his breathing ragged and uneven. They were silent for a long moment, breathing each other's air, sharing each other's strength. Phoebe waited; she knew what she wanted from Leo, but she didn't want to ask. She'd trust instead.

'I love you,' Leo finally murmured; it was a confession. Phoebe closed her eyes in relief. 'I love you,' he said again, stronger now, 'but I never thought you could— truly—love me.'

'I do.'

Leo shook his head, pulling away a little bit. 'I can hardly believe it. There's no reason—'

'I told you the reasons.' Phoebe pulled him closer again, and brushed his lips with hers. 'Although I dare say I can think of a few more.'

Leo kissed her back, a slow and lingering kiss, a kiss that swept away the memories and fears, the guilt and regret, and left only its clean, pure beauty.

Phoebe closed her eyes, resting her cheek against Leo's shoulder, felt the solid comfort of his presence, the joy of his love. Outside the sun had set, and moonlight glittered on the snow. The day had ended, a long, endless day, a day that held years of sorrow and pain in it. That day, she thought as Leo claimed her mouth in a kiss once more, was past.

A new day had begun.

EPILOGUE

IT WAS a beautiful April day, the air crisp and clean, the sky washed a perfect robin's-egg blue after the morning rain. Phoebe stood to the left of Leo, her hand clasped with Christian's, smiling through the misty veil of tears. Happy tears.

Christian wriggled, impatient and uncomfortable in his heavy robe. Phoebe sympathised; her own gown was twenty yards of embroidered satin that had been worn by the last eleven queens of Amarnes…the title she was about to assume, as soon as Leo was crowned.

She watched with pride and joy as the archbishop placed the heavy, ancient crown on his head, the sapphires and rubies sparkling in the sunlight. A cheer rose from the crowd in a swell of pride and joy, an outpouring of love for their new king.

Phoebe had seen it these last few months, felt it whenever she'd gone out in Njardvik. Old women pressed her hand and conferred silent blessings; children brought ragged posies of flowers. Everyone was delighted Leo was king. They were ready for a good king, a loving king. They were ready for King Leopold I.

The ancient rite concluded, Phoebe stepped forward to

accept her own crown, glad she'd used her hair-straightening serum for once, even though Leo liked her hair wild and curly. The crown sat on her smooth knot of hair, huge and heavy, yet it was a weight she bore gladly.

As another prayer was offered for the monarchs' long and prosperous reign, Leo's hand found Phoebe's, his fingers twining with hers.

'All right?' he whispered, glancing in concern at the slight swell of Phoebe's belly. She smiled back at him, one hand coming as it had months before to rest on her middle, almost as if she could feel the pulse of new life with her fingers.

'More than all right,' she whispered back. Another cheer rose from the crowd and, as one, Phoebe and Leo turned to greet their people. 'More than all right,' Phoebe repeated as joy swelled inside her. Christian wriggled his way as he often did to be between them, one hand clasped with each of theirs. 'More, even,' Phoebe whispered, 'than wonderful.' Leo glanced at her, one eyebrow arched, a smile hovering about his mouth so Phoebe knew he agreed completely.

Yes, more than wonderful, she thought…in fact, just about perfect.

MILLS & BOON

SEPTEMBER 2009 HARDBACK TITLES

ROMANCE

A Bride for His Majesty's Pleasure	Penny Jordan
The Master Player	Emma Darcy
The Infamous Italian's Secret Baby	Carole Mortimer
The Millionaire's Christmas Wife	Helen Brooks
Duty, Desire and the Desert King	Jane Porter
Royal Love-Child, Forbidden Marriage	Kate Hewitt
One-Night Mistress...Convenient Wife	Anne McAllister
Prince of Montéz, Pregnant Mistress	Sabrina Philips
The Count of Castelfino	Christina Hollis
Beauty and the Billionaire	Barbara Dunlop
Crowned: The Palace Nanny	Marion Lennox
Christmas Angel for the Billionaire	Liz Fielding
Under the Boss's Mistletoe	Jessica Hart
Jingle-Bell Baby	Linda Goodnight
The Magic of a Family Christmas	Susan Meier
Mistletoe & Marriage	Patricia Thayer & Donna Alward
Her Baby Out of the Blue	Alison Roberts
A Doctor, A Nurse: A Christmas Baby	Amy Andrews

HISTORICAL

Devilish Lord, Mysterious Miss	Annie Burrows
To Kiss a Count	Amanda McCabe
The Earl and the Governess	Sarah Elliott

MEDICAL™

Country Midwife, Christmas Bride	Abigail Gordon
Greek Doctor: One Magical Christmas	Meredith Webber
Spanish Doctor, Pregnant Midwife	Anne Fraser
Expecting a Christmas Miracle	Laura Iding

0809 Gen Std LP

SEPTEMBER 2009 LARGE PRINT TITLES

ROMANCE

The Sicilian Boss's Mistress	Penny Jordan
Pregnant with the Billionaire's Baby	Carole Mortimer
The Venadicci Marriage Vengeance	Melanie Milburne
The Ruthless Billionaire's Virgin	Susan Stephens
Italian Tycoon, Secret Son	Lucy Gordon
Adopted: Family in a Million	Barbara McMahon
The Billionaire's Baby	Nicola Marsh
Blind-Date Baby	Fiona Harper

HISTORICAL

Lord Braybrook's Penniless Bride	Elizabeth Rolls
A Country Miss in Hanover Square	Anne Herries
Chosen for the Marriage Bed	Anne O'Brien

MEDICAL™

The Children's Doctor's Special Proposal	Kate Hardy
English Doctor, Italian Bride	Carol Marinelli
The Doctor's Baby Bombshell	Jennifer Taylor
Emergency: Single Dad, Mother Needed	Laura Iding
The Doctor Claims His Bride	Fiona Lowe
Assignment: Baby	Lynne Marshall

0909 Gen Std HB

OCTOBER 2009 HARDBACK TITLES

ROMANCE

The Billionaire's Bride of Innocence	Miranda Lee
Dante: Claiming His Secret Love-Child	Sandra Marton
The Sheikh's Impatient Virgin	Kim Lawrence
His Forbidden Passion	Anne Mather
The Mistress of His Manor	Catherine George
Ruthless Greek Boss, Secretary Mistress	Abby Green
Cavelli's Lost Heir	Lynn Raye Harris
The Blackmail Baby	Natalie Rivers
Da Silva's Mistress	Tina Duncan
The Twelve-Month Marriage Deal	Margaret Mayo
And the Bride Wore Red	Lucy Gordon
Her Desert Dream	Liz Fielding
Their Christmas Family Miracle	Caroline Anderson
Snowbound Bride-to-Be	Cara Colter
Her Mediterranean Makeover	Claire Baxter
Confidential: Expecting!	Jackie Braun
Snowbound: Miracle Marriage	Sarah Morgan
Christmas Eve: Doorstep Delivery	Sarah Morgan

HISTORICAL

Compromised Miss	Anne O'Brien
The Wayward Governess	Joanna Fulford
Runaway Lady, Conquering Lord	Carol Townend

MEDICAL™

Hot-Shot Doc, Christmas Bride	Joanna Neil
Christmas at Rivercut Manor	Gill Sanderson
Falling for the Playboy Millionaire	Kate Hardy
The Surgeon's New-Year Wedding Wish	Laura Iding

0909 Gen Std LP

OCTOBER 2009 LARGE PRINT TITLES

ROMANCE

The Billionaire's Bride of Convenience	Miranda Lee
Valentino's Love-Child	Lucy Monroe
Ruthless Awakening	Sara Craven
The Italian Count's Defiant Bride	Catherine George
Outback Heiress, Surprise Proposal	Margaret Way
Honeymoon with the Boss	Jessica Hart
His Princess in the Making	Melissa James
Dream Date with the Millionaire	Melissa McClone

HISTORICAL

His Reluctant Mistress	Joanna Maitland
The Earl's Forbidden Ward	Bronwyn Scott
The Rake's Inherited Courtesan	Ann Lethbridge

MEDICAL™

A Family For His Tiny Twins	Josie Metcalfe
One Night With Her Boss	Alison Roberts
Top-Notch Doc, Outback Bride	Melanie Milburne
A Baby for the Village Doctor	Abigail Gordon
The Midwife and the Single Dad	Gill Sanderson
The Playboy Firefighter's Proposal	Emily Forbes

millsandboon.co.uk Community

Join Us!

The Community is the perfect place to meet and chat to kindred spirits who love books and reading as much as you do, but it's also the place to:

- **Get the inside scoop from authors about their latest books**
- **Learn how to write a romance book with advice from our editors**
- **Help us to continue publishing the best in women's fiction**
- **Share your thoughts on the books we publish**
- **Befriend other users**

Forums: Interact with each other as well as authors, editor and a whole host of other users worldwide.

Blogs: Every registered community member has their own blog to tell the world what they're up to and what's on their mind.

Book Challenge: We're aiming to read 5,000 books and have joined forces with The Reading Agency in our inaugural Book Challenge.

Profile Page: Showcase yourself and keep a record of you recent community activity.

Social Networking: We've added buttons at the end of every post to share via digg, Facebook, Google, Yahoo, technorati and de.licio.us.

www.millsandboon.co.uk

MILLS & BOON®

www.millsandboon.co.uk

- All the latest titles
- Free online reads
- Irresistible special offers

And there's more…

- Missed a book? Buy from our huge discounted backlist
- Sign up to our FREE monthly eNewsletter
- eBooks available now
- More about your favourite authors
- Great competitions

Make sure you visit today!

www.millsandboon.co.uk